"I have to wear i tomorrow night, so don't rip it off, okay?"

Cameron sat up and gave Tess the sweetest smile. "I have *never* in my life ripped clothes off a woman. Undressing is foreplay. Why miss out on that?"

His hand traveled up her leg, beneath the silken skirt and rested for a moment on her hip. One teasing finger slipped beneath the strap at the side of her thong. His lazy gaze never left hers.

Tess saw right into his mind in that instant as if he had opened up to her on purpose, an offering of trust, a gift. She saw raw anticipation. She saw all that he imagined they would do together. She saw need that stretched beyond the night. Tantalizing. And erotic.

Slowly he removed his hand from beneath the dress, caressing her leg as he began to lift the hem. When he drew it over her head and carefully laid it aside, Tess shivered with eagerness....

Dear Reader,

Here's what happens when an idealistic, by-the-book agent with little experience meets a seasoned operative who has battled burnout, the bad guys and also the bureaucracy that put him in place. Cameron lost the last round, but has a second chance on all fronts if he chooses to accept the challenge.

The ability to adapt to the situation plays a crucial role in an undercover operative's work. He or she often has to assume a persona that doesn't quite fit. Is it possible, in the acting out of the part, to discover hidden corners of the personality that conceal unexpected traits? Tess and Cameron will find out. Surprises are in store as the op brings out the best and worst of both.

Perhaps The Big Reveal is just as well for two people falling head over heels against all the rules and their better judgment. Love will lay it all on the line in *The Agent's Proposition*.

Join the ride. It's bound to be wild!

Lyn Stone

LYN STONE

The Agent's Proposition

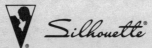

Romantic
SUSPENSE

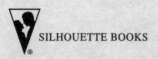 SILHOUETTE BOOKS

ISBN-13: 978-0-373-27662-2

Recycling programs
for this product may
not exist in your area.

THE AGENT'S PROPOSITION

Books by Lyn Stone

Silhouette Romantic Suspense
Beauty and the Badge #952
Live-In Lover #1055
A Royal Murder #1172
In Harm's Way #1193
Down to the Wire #1281
Against the Wall #1295
Under the Gun #1330
Straight Through the Heart #1408
From Mission to Marriage #1444
Special Agent's Seduction #1449
Kiss or Kill #1488
The Doctor's Mission #1534
Claimed by the Secret Agent #1552
The Agent's Proposition #1592

*Special Ops

LYN STONE

is a former artist who developed an early and avid interest in criminology while helping her husband study for his degree. His subsequent career in counterintelligence and his contacts in the field provided a built-in source for research in writing suspense. Their long and happy marriage provided firsthand knowledge of happily-ever-afters.

This book is dedicated to my good friend
Shauna Keenon, one courageous lady.

Prologue

McLean, Virginia

"Sir, why in the world would you want to hire this man for our team?" Tess Bradshaw demanded. "Look at this last performance appraisal!" She thumped the page for emphasis as she read aloud. "*Employs unorthodox methods, ignores rules and regulations.* I can see why the CIA branded him a rogue and forced him to resign."

Jack Mercier shrugged. "We need him, at least temporarily. So convince him to come on board."

Tess tossed the page on the desk, sat back in her chair and crossed her arms, shaking her head as she did. "Does he have any special abilities?"

Each of the agents on the SEXTANT and COMPASS

teams had some edge that made them and the units special, like a photographic mind, a phenomenal ear for languages or psychic skills. Tess was an empath. Maybe she shouldn't have mentioned Cochran's lack of an edge, since her own wasn't all that well honed yet. She was still amazed to find herself a member of a civilian special ops team specializing in counterintelligence.

"He's a good hacker and extremely proficient at physically following up on what he finds. He's excellent at infiltrating, adapting and anticipating. Also speaks three languages fluently. Not unusual for our teams, but remarkable enough."

"Are we after the same group who threatened the Bulk Power System eighteen months ago? Could it be Al Qaeda?"

"Maybe. We do know they have detailed schematics for our power facilities. But this threat is virtually identical to the last one, when they cut the power for almost all the eastern seaboard. Cyber Security managed to override their control within a few hours, but this new threat is more sophisticated."

"All the agencies are on this, I bet."

"Working all fronts. The NSA tracked the origin of the e-mails to a general location but is unable to pinpoint the actual source. Maybe Cochran can zero in on it. He did last time and was ready to apprehend. The Company jumped the gun and botched his efforts, then shifted the blame to Cochran. I hope this chance for redemption will prompt Cochran to join us, at least for this op."

"What if he's bitter, or just not interested?" she asked.

"Then you will have failed *your* mission, Agent

Bradshaw. *Get* him interested. We have only a week before the lights go out." He handed her another file with the details of the earlier case and added a smaller folder of travel documents. "You'll find him on Tybee Island on the Georgia coast." He tapped the new folder with one finger. "His passport, credentials and a badge. Don't let go of these unless he agrees to do this."

"I'll convince him," she declared. Orders were orders. "Where will he be going on the op?"

Mercier stood up, her signal that the briefing was over. "The French Riviera. Better buy yourself a new bikini and some sunscreen when you land in Savannah."

"What? Why?"

"Because you're going with him."

Chapter 1

Tybee Island, Georgia

Cameron Cochran lounged on the deck of the *Lucky Duck,* his thirty-one-foot Morgan powerboat. Café Loco looked too busy for him to go over there for beer, and he was down to his last one.

He propped his bare feet on the rail and rubbed the surviving cold bottle of Dos Equis across the middle of his chest to cool off. It was damned hot for early October, even for Georgia.

In another few weeks he planned to knock off for the year. The fishing business was slow anyway. He hadn't had the boat out of the creek and in open water for three days. A good many of the neighboring slips were empty today, but most of them advertised, did tours, catered to tourists. He took only small groups of two or three who seriously liked to fish.

Tomorrow's client was late in coming by with the deposit, and he had a good mind to go ahead and leave. Might as well finish the beer. He took a swig and sighed.

Life was good here. He still had that feeling something was missing, though. Maybe the high he got when all his senses were revved and the safety was off. Maybe a little passion for what he was doing. Maybe a little passion, period.

Cameron grunted at the maudlin thought and took another swallow, enjoying the cool brew. He had it made. What fool wouldn't love to be doing what he was doing, bunking on a sweet little craft and fishing for a living?

Most nights he didn't even bother going to the house. It was just a place to keep the stuff he didn't have room for on the *Duck.*

A tapping sound caught his attention. *Ah, that must be tomorrow's fare, strutting down the dock in high heels and a skirt.* He'd bet this one wouldn't be baiting any hooks. She looked cute, though, in a tightly wound, bean-counter kind of way. The bigger outfits must be sending him the ones they didn't want to fool with.

She had her little beige suit coat draped over one arm, and perspiration molded her bright blue slip top to her skin. Damp strands of dark blond hair had escaped the prim little bun and clung to her temples.

"Are you Cameron Cochran?" she asked, shielding her brow with her hand.

"Ms. Bradshaw." He knew who she was. He recognized her voice from the phone call a few hours earlier. She had left a message, asking to meet with him at 2:00 p.m. It was almost three-thirty. "You're late."

"My flight was delayed. Weather," she explained with an impatient shake of her head. "May I, uh, come on the boat?" She stood near the edge of the dock, eyeing the gentle lap of waves against the pilings. She looked worried.

"Take your shoes off," he ordered. Reluctantly, he set down his beer and got up to help her board. Probably couldn't make it by herself since her skirt was so slim-fitting. He finally just grabbed her by the waist and hefted her over and onto the deck.

She brushed his hands off as if he'd been handling fish. Cameron smiled down at her, enjoying himself. She was a pretty little thing and obviously way out of her comfort zone.

He stood back, hands on his hips. "Okay, here's the deal. We'll leave around six in the morning and go out about twenty miles. Depending on what we find, we should get a few sea bass, flounder, snapper or mackerel. If you feel adventurous, we could try for barracuda."

"I didn't come to fish," she announced, straightening her skirt.

He glanced pointedly around the marina and back at her. "Well, honey, this *is* a fishing boat, and that's about all I do. You want a tour, there're boats for that."

She held out her hand for him to shake. "I'm Agent Tess Bradshaw, and I work for SEXTANT. Our director, Special Agent Jack Mercier, sent me to offer you a position with our team. I know you worked for the CIA, so I'm sure you know who we are."

Cameron froze, pinning her with a glare. She drew up to her full height of about five-four and glared back. "Look, I know that was direct, but I saw no point in engaging in a lot of small talk before delivering the offer. The pay is good, and you'll have a chance to get at that hacker again. No interference this time and Mercier will have your file completely wiped of all the accusations made against you before you left the Company."

"Get off my boat," Cameron growled. All the bitterness he thought he'd conquered flooded back.

"Wait, please!"

"For what? I'm done."

She cleared her throat and stepped away when he would have lifted her back onto the dock. "I could lose my job if you say no."

"Good. You'll be better off." He reached for her again, but she dodged him.

"Listen to me, will you?" Wide-eyed, probably afraid of him, she backed up to the far rail, dropped her shoes and held on with both hands. "We need you. Your country needs you. There's another threat to the B.P.S. The mitigating effort's not working. They want money, or they'll strike."

He so didn't want to get into this again. "One more hour and I would have had the man. The Company rushed in, screwed my mission, then blamed me when it failed."

"Mercier knows that."

Cameron didn't care. "If they need a standby scapegoat this time, they can damn well find somebody else."

"You got a raw deal. Mercier will rectify that if you'll only help us out with this one mission. It's one you worked on for nearly a year! Here's your opportunity to make it happen your way. Take it, Cochran."

"Tell him to fix my record, get me an official apology in writing and I'll think about it." Cameron would *think,* as promised, but he wouldn't *do.* Her expression said she guessed as much. *Smart cookie.*

He sat back down in his chair and picked up his beer.

The persistent little devil didn't budge. "We know where he is. He has been traced to a general area but has moved too much within it to be pinpointed precisely," she told him. "Intel says he's contacted the Department of Energy with a demand for millions. You know the government policy on extortion, so it's only a matter of time…."

Cameron swiped his forehead with the side of his bottle, now too warm to do any good. "You have a location, so go in and throw a wide net."

He hated the prickle of anticipation he was feeling. And the itch to participate, damn it. He wanted to so badly, he could taste it, despite the bitterness. Or maybe because of that. Would he ever have another chance like this to clear his name?

She held his gaze, probably knew she had him already, even as she spoke. "The evidence would disappear in a blink if we used a traditional approach. That's what happened last time, right? Mercier says you'd be lead on the mission and we do things your way. And if you want employment with our team after we succeed, he will seriously consider it."

Was it possible somebody actually believed he was innocent? Enough to hire him? In any case, they sure knew how to tempt him. "What's with the *we?* Who else is on it?"

She dropped her gaze to her feet, then looked up at him through her lashes and frowned. "Me."

Cameron laughed out loud. He stopped suddenly and sighed. "Who goes if I refuse? Just you?"

She shrugged and nodded.

Okay, there was his justification for sticking his head back in the noose. Damn it, he couldn't let her try to handle this on her own. Young as she looked, she couldn't have much experience.

This could prove really dangerous if it involved a serious criminal element and not just some greedy hacker testing his skills.

Her carefully blank expression and lack of any telling body language indicated she could be lying about taking this on by herself. But what if she wasn't? Intel personnel had to be stretched pretty thin across the board these days with so many cuts in funding. They might send her out alone, thinking there would be little chance of physical danger involved.

"Please reconsider," she said. "I know how much that last op cost you. Think about it, Cochran. Here's your chance to turn that around."

She couldn't know all he had lost. That wouldn't be in his record for her to read. Some things couldn't be turned around no matter what he did. Like Brenda.

She had deserted him the minute she found out he'd been forced to leave the Company. Losing her was probably the only stroke of good fortune associated with his fall from grace, but at the time he hadn't seen it that way. He had needed love and support. He had gotten a halfhearted apology and his ring back.

Even that was more than his family had offered. His dad, still disgruntled about Cameron's career choice, had muttered a pointed "I told you so" and extended a grudging job offer. Cameron's polite refusal had nearly cut all ties with his parents, but he could not see himself as an accountant making his bones in order to inherit Daddy's firm eventually. This was *his* life, damn it.

Now even his mother thought he was a bum and wore a look of despair every time he visited. They lived less than ten miles away, and he, an only child and the black sheep, rarely saw either of them. His weekly call to check on their health and say hello was both bittersweet and excruciating.

Yeah, he had lost, all right, but he still had his self-respect and his independence. He made a fair living and answered to nobody. Could he give that up on the off chance he could prove he was a good agent? Even if he succeeded, who was left to care?

Who was he kidding? *He* cared. He damn well cared.

The sudden leap of hope made him furious with himself. And with her, for causing it. He hated the reminder of what he had once been and what he was now. How many times had he dreamed of being called back, being needed to do what no other agent could, and of saying a nonchalant "no thanks" to the ones who had betrayed him?

Now he faced a decision, welcome revenge or a chance at redemption. What if he took the chance and failed? What if, again, they engineered his failure?

She watched him, her expression hopeful.

Even if he wanted to say yes, what could he do with his hands tied? "I can't leave the country. The authorities lifted my papers and warned me not to."

"Taken care of. Passport, badge and credentials, Everything you'll need. You also get your CRYPTO clearance back. C'mon, you get carte blanche."

Cameron put down the warm beer again and stood up. So much for his sense of self-preservation. He needed to ditch his pride and do this. *Had* to, and not just to keep her out of trouble, he admitted. There might never be another opportunity for him to set things straight. "I'll need a few days to make arrangements for my business here."

"I'm sorry, but this has a short fuse. We have to leave today. I'll do whatever I can to help you get ready." She was obviously grateful and relieved he was in, but the offer sounded a little stiff in spite of that. He suspected she hadn't agreed with her boss's orders to recruit him. She sure deserved a solid A for effort, though. She had set the hook and reeled him in.

That uptight attitude had to loosen up a little if they were going to get along at all. He grabbed the shirt hanging over the arm of his chair and pulled it on, then stepped into his deck shoes. "My car's up at the café. Let's go."

"Where?" she asked. "You're not planning to drive anywhere, are you?" She glanced pointedly at the discarded beer bottle. "You've been drinking."

"Half a beer doesn't affect me." He beckoned her to his side of the deck and lifted her onto the dock. She yelped a little when he almost dropped her on purpose.

"I'm driving!" she declared when he joined her.

"Suit yourself."

He led the way up to the parking lot and waited for her as she paid her fare and sent the waiting cab on its way back to town. When she rejoined him, he ushered her into the café and hailed Bobby Ray, who was sitting at the bar, sucking down a draft. "Hey, take over for me for a couple of weeks, will you?"

"Yeah, sure, no problem," Bobby Ray muttered.

Cameron tossed him the keys to the boat. "Hire a mate. Don't take her out by yourself. Tomorrow's still open. Take care of the *Duck* for me, or I'll wring your skinny neck."

Bobby Ray nodded and pocketed the keys. He never said much. Clients probably didn't enjoy his company, but he was careful on the water and damn good at finding fish.

"Are you sure you can trust him?" she asked as they were leaving the café. "He looks sort of…disreputable."

He did at that. Scrawny, dressed like a bum, rarely shaved, missing a few teeth. But he was a good man. Cameron inclined his head and took her arm to guide the little agent to his car. "We're a disreputable lot, and that's a fact, ma'am, but we look out for each other. And I have really good insurance."

"Don't call me *ma'am*."

"It's a Southern thing, sign of respect."

"You don't know me. How do you know I deserve respect?" she snapped.

"Call me an optimist." He stopped beside the Chevy, opened the passenger door and got in. The window was already down, so he reached out and handed her the key. "Here you go."

She took the key ring and stared at it, frowning.

"So, you driving or what?" he asked, prompting her to get a move on. If they had a short fuse on this like she said, they needed to get busy.

She hurried around the rust-spotted hood and got in. After a cursory assessment of the interior, she remarked, "There aren't any seat belts."

"Or air-conditioning. She's an old car. We have to go only about two miles, though. You'll be safe enough."

She stuck the key in the ignition and twisted it. Cameron smiled at the deafening rumble. Who needed a muffler to go two miles? He rarely drove anywhere but to the house and back.

"Hit the main drag and hang a right."

There were no more comments about his ride, and he gave her points for that. He had bought the clunker from Bobby Ray for a couple of hundred when the boy had needed money.

"Are we going to your house?" she asked, shifting gears rather expertly.

"Yep. Turn right here. Third house on the left." He pointed to a small clapboard cottage with blue shutters.

"Cute," Bradshaw commented as she parked in the shell-scattered driveway. "I'll just wait in the car."

"Come on in. You know you're curious." He shot her a daring grin. As long as he was committed to doing this, he might as well make up his mind to enjoy it.

Without further argument, she got out of the car and followed him inside.

"Make yourself comfortable while I pack."

"All right," she said, perching on the edge of the old sofa, elbows resting on her knees, hands clasped. She surveyed the room with a critical eye. "Is this where you grew up?"

"Nope. Savannah. This was my granddaddy's place. Now mine."

"Does your family still live in Savannah?"

"Yeah. If you want something cold to drink, there's tea in the fridge. Help yourself." He left her there.

"So this is your retirement home?" she called out from the living room.

"I don't *have* a retirement," he snapped, wishing the bitter words back the instant they were out.

"That could change if this works out. You could move back to the D.C. area."

He didn't answer, because he didn't know what to say. Pride wouldn't let him admit to her that he wished he could get his old life back, square things with his superiors and regain his father's respect. Until she made the offer, he hadn't realized how desperately he wanted that. Yeah, he would go and he would succeed this time no matter what it took.

Half the country could suffer a power outage if he didn't. A shutdown across the power grid could cause deaths and seriously impact critical infrastructures. The economy, in rough shape now, would tank completely. Clearing his name meant a lot to him, all right. And, of course, there was little Agent Bradshaw, who might run into trouble and get herself hurt or worse if he refused.

Enough analyzing. He had made a decision and that was that. He had never been one for second-guessing himself. Fully committed was the only way he knew to approach things. Full steam ahead.

Packing was simple enough. She had said the source of this threat was not in country, so he ought to prepare for any contingency. He included his tux and accoutrements, his best suit and the expensive casual things he hadn't used since his last undercover gig in London. He added the forbidden laptop. Had they really thought he'd abide by that directive?

On the off chance that Bradshaw wasn't providing equipment for him, he tossed in a pack of disposable wrist restraints, a penlight, his knife and his Kevlar vest. The Glock went in the bag next, along with his .38 caliber backup.

He didn't bother to change clothes, since she was in such a hurry. So was he, now that he'd agreed to do this.

She was sipping a glass of tea without ice when he reentered the living room. "Come on. Make it quick."

"You're in a rush all of a sudden," she said as they walked to the car.

"Might as well get this show on the road. By the way, where are we going?" he asked.

"France. The Riviera."

"That covers a good bit of ground."

"Saint Tropez. Are you familiar with it?"

"Oh, yeah. Interesting beaches," he replied with a suggestive smile, knowing full well she'd start picturing all the sunbathers nude. Some of them would be, maybe *most* of them. How would Miss Prim and Proper react to that reality? He had to admit he wouldn't mind seeing her try to blend in with the locals on one of those beaches.

She seemed a little too "by the book" to be working for such an offbeat agency. The bunch at SEXTANT were supposed to have psychic leanings, at least according to the scuttlebutt at the Company. The agents had joked about it.

Cameron hadn't joked. He had been raised in Savannah, where psychics lived on every corner and were nothing to laugh at. He was no fortune-teller or mind reader, but he had experienced a few premonitions himself, so he didn't discount things of that nature. The government had been implementing special programs exploring psychic phenomena for decades. Maybe they had come up with something useful, after all.

However, he figured if Bradshaw were able to read his mind, she wouldn't have had to ask so many questions.

Also, she wouldn't be so worried about whether she could trust him to do what he'd agreed to do. She would also know the Cochran agenda stretched past protecting the power grid and establishing his innocence. Now that he'd made the decision to take this on, his former ultimate goal had returned with renewed determination.

Cameron wanted the guy he had almost caught, but that was just the first step. Somebody else was calling the shots. He was sure of it. An insider, an American, a traitor.

He looked at Agent Bradshaw more objectively than he had before and tried to judge how she might react to a life-threatening situation. She must be pretty well trained and fairly intelligent to get where she was in the business, but she looked so damned innocent and untried.

He hoped she would be able to handle what was coming, because traitors, when cornered, could potentially prove lethal. They had nothing left to lose by fighting to the death.

Then again, now that he thought about it, neither did he.

Chapter 2

Tess evaluated what she knew about Cochran. He looked a darn sight different in person than in his official photo. What had not been captured by the camera was the laid-back sexuality, which sort of drew you in if you weren't careful. Like a spell or something...

Cochran scared her a little. Not physically, but he threatened her self-confidence when it came to judging men. He probably wasn't what he seemed, so what was he?

The photo in the file showed a perfectly groomed, rather handsome government agent wearing a gray suit, a short haircut and a stern expression. In person, at first meeting, he'd been a half-naked, wildly attractive sea captain with a killer tan and a sun-bleached mane that needed a trim. That lazy grin, combined with his intense green-eyed appraisal of her, had raised the hairs on her arms. Still did.

He made eye contact readily enough, but she was the one uncomfortable with it, not him. And she couldn't read a thing he was thinking.

Maybe this *was* the real Cochran. Maybe getting fired had changed him. It was impossible to know who she was dealing with here, and that bothered her a lot.

The Company had confiscated his computers and fearing he would retaliate against them by using his expertise, had ordered him not to replace them. She would bet he'd gotten around the directive in short order and really hoped he had. Technology changed so rapidly, he'd be well behind the curve now if he hadn't kept up.

She noted he hadn't bothered to change out of his shorts, Café Loco shirt and deck shoes. Once she'd told him about the private jet waiting for them, he had seemed eager get on with it.

They were in the air now, and Cochran had been on her cell phone with Mercier for the last half hour, working out the specifics of their deal and details on the case.

Tess felt a little out of the loop, but she was glad her first mission had been accomplished. When she'd made the call for Cochran, Mercier had congratulated her and wished her well on her first real assignment in the field. She had been on backup for three others since he had hired her, and apparently he now trusted her to go secondary on this one.

Six years ago Tess had felt confident enough in her skill, and admittedly curious enough, to volunteer for a small study in parapsychology sponsored by the University of Virginia where she was enrolled. She learned later that the study was actually a renamed and privately funded continuation of the CIA's Star Gate Project, which had been officially launched in the 1970s.

The study primarily involved remote viewing, which could aid in producing intelligence data. But her particular skills must have been recorded, because four years later she had been recruited.

She had qualified her skill when describing it to Mercier, but he had seemed satisfied that she would be a valuable member of the team and had hired her.

This was her first time out without a fellow SEXTANT agent in the lead on a case. Tess wished she knew Cochran better than she did. She didn't like not knowing exactly who had her back.

There was the sexual attraction, which she would have to deal with, too. She had felt something like it before, but that had come to no good in a great big hurry.

Brian had been her first and only, the perfect choice—or so she had thought at the time. Early on Tess had decided to wait for love to have sex. She had to make her own rules, and that one had seemed prudent at the time. As a result, she'd reached her sophomore year in college virtually untouched.

He had been so attentive, so persuasive and so handsome. She hadn't even tried to read his thoughts, thinking that would be intrusive and somehow taking advantage of him. She should have asked herself why a great-looking, popular jock like him, with so many other choices available, would attach himself to a bookish little mouse like her.

Maybe in the back of her mind, she *had* questioned it. But she hadn't wanted to analyze the way she felt or look any deeper into his intentions. Starry-eyed and infatuated, she had accepted all his words of undying love as absolute devotion. Until the day after she'd given in to it completely. He had told everyone, leaving her humiliated.

She looked up as Cameron returned to the seat beside her and handed her back the phone. "I got all the details of the investigation so far. Mercier's arranging for a yacht we can stay on, a repo that's small enough we can crew it, but big enough to impress."

"A boat? Jack's putting us on a boat? Why?"

"Because I suggested it. Our target is moving. Could be on water, so we ought to be prepared for that. He agreed it was a good idea."

Tess hated boats. She had quailed at boarding Cochran's back on Tybee. But she wasn't about to reveal her nearly phobic fear to Cochran. That was no way to begin.

He pinned her again with that intense scrutiny, as if he were trying to read her thoughts.

She knew that look. Was *he* psychic? She couldn't read him. That had bothered her when they met, but she hadn't worried too much. She could read some people, but they had to be open to it, either willing to let her or clueless about her trying. He didn't strike her as either willing or clueless.

"You don't like boats," he stated, guessing. Or maybe he *knew.*

"I don't have any experience with them, that's all. You'll have to teach me what to do."

"Don't worry about it. You'll be an old salt in no time."

That remained to be seen. "Why can't we stay in one of the hotels?"

He sighed and pinched the bridge of his nose. "Because once we find this dude, we have to get him into international waters to arrest him."

"No, we don't. The French police will cooperate with us. They have before. Jack has influence, and jurisdiction shouldn't be a problem at all."

"Yeah, they'll hold whomever we catch, maybe even let us interrogate him, but under their collective thumb. Trust me, we won't have the time to cut through bureaucracy. We need to get this guy and find out who he's working for immediately. His boss might have a backup hacker and go right ahead with his plan."

"His boss?"

"He's not working this alone. Also, if we don't have our perp isolated, who do you think he'll contact the minute he gets to a phone or a computer?" He stared straight into her eyes. "Get over the boat thing. I know what I'm doing."

"I hope you do." This was just another battle she would have to fight in order to be who she wanted to be. She had won others, like conquering her strong resistance to confrontation and her aversion to physical contact. She admitted she still overcompensated to some degree, but for the most part, she was well over those hurdles and felt pretty good about herself.

She had overcome her childhood, or rather her lack of one. Her parents had been reared in a commune until they rebelled and ran away at seventeen. Their awkward attempts at entering the establishment had thrust a lot of responsibility onto the daughter they'd had too early in their lives.

Impulse had governed them and probably always would, but not Tess, who had a firm grip on reality, knew how to map her success and conquer her fears. So, she wasn't about to quail at riding in a stupid boat.

"Nice plane," he commented, looking around as if he hadn't noticed before. "Not exactly Air Force One, but nice. Does it have a shower?"

"Back there," she replied, pointing, hoping he would fit into the little enclosure. He was a large man, well over six feet tall and well muscled, almost bulked like a weight lifter. Deep-sea fishing must provide a great workout.

She jerked her gaze away from his legs, bare from just above his knees to below his ankles. He had great legs. She cleared her throat, hoping he hadn't noticed her noticing. "Your bag—"

"I know where it is. I stowed it." He got up and smiled down at her. "I'll just go and clean up a little."

Tess nodded, wondering if he would be in there long enough for her to snoop. Had he brought a weapon? A computer? Anything else she should know about?

"Will we have to go through customs?" he asked, as if he'd read her mind. Again.

"No. Mercier called ahead. He…knows people," she stammered. "Do you have a weapon?"

"Two, which I wouldn't want confiscated, and I don't like anyone touching my laptop."

Tess dropped her gaze, knowing it might reflect the

guilt she felt about her plan to search his things. "You're not supposed to have a computer."

He laughed at that, and the sound of his laughter stroked every cell in her body as he left her to take his shower.

Damn, the man rattled her. She had to get over it and get her composure back. Her uncanny instincts didn't work when she was this unnerved, and they *had* to work.

At least she had gotten him on board the mission and had accomplished her initial goal. She had to relinquish control of the op to him now, and that would be the most difficult aspect of the job.

Tess liked being in charge, but she had to admit this was not the time, any more than on the last two missions. Gaining experience had to take precedence. She had lied a little bit, indicating that Mercier would have sent her on alone if Cochran had refused to join her, but he didn't have to know that.

She leaned back in her seat and tried to relax, regroup and unwind. All she could think about was that wicked smile of his, which mocked even as it dared, judged even as it flattered. What a puzzle Cochran was. *Cameron.* Would they progress to a first-name basis? Did she even want to?

She closed her eyes and tried to imagine the two of them working in tandem, as partners, maybe even friends. Could she unbend enough to manage a friendship? Certainly never *more* than that, she warned herself, no matter how heart-stopping he looked or how powerful that spell of his turned out to be.

His touch, innocent at it had been the few times they had made contact, had alarmed and upset her. She couldn't allow herself to backslide and become the scared little rabbit she had been growing up.

All those stories her mom had told about the evils of free love and rampant sex in the commune hadn't helped Tess develop well socially. They had created yet another fear to be conquered. Next time she would be the one to initiate contact. She would do the touching, she decided, and she wouldn't let it shake her, either. Not one little bit.

It could work with guys. It could work with boats. It was only a matter of employing systematic desensitization and cognitive restructuring of thoughts and misconceptions. She knew how to get over these things.

He returned to his seat half an hour later. Transformed. Tess was speechless. And more rattled than ever. His suit was a tropical beige, jet-set expensive, as were his Italian loafers and the dark brown V-necked pullover. Cashmere, she was certain. The Rolex watch, signet ring and diamond ear stud must have set him back a fortune, too.

"What's the matter? Did I miss a spot?" He stroked his chin with two fingers.

"N-no. You look…fine." *Oh, man. Too fine,* she thought with a sigh.

He raked her with an assessing look. "Your turn. Did you bring anything less…austere? I'm afraid you look just like an agent should, and we can't have that."

His southern accent had disappeared, and his speech sounded more like that of a newscaster. How'd he do that?

Tess was still trying to come to grips with the change in his appearance as she shook her head. All she could think of were her plain, low-heeled pumps—in beige, which went with everything—and her neat little suits from JC Penney. She frowned down at the Timex ticking away on her wrist. She felt…positively plebeian.

"Well, don't worry about it," he said. "We can fix that after we land."

"Fix what?" she muttered.

"You," he said, then shrugged. "Your wardrobe. The hair. Makeup. You'll need to get in step for when we hit the clubs, maybe even the casinos."

"Casinos?"

"Yeah, we'll check the clubs in Saint-Tropez first, but the casinos are where we're probably going to find him."

"How would you know that?"

Cochran smiled and raised his eyebrows. "Because I know who we're after, and he loves to gamble."

Tess thought he was blowing smoke. Yet he radiated confidence like a space heater. Her doubt must be showing, because he continued without waiting for her to comment.

"Mercier related the message letter for letter when I asked, and I recognized the signature misspellings. There's also a cadence and tone to it that are familiar. This guy's wordy. And English is not his first language. This is the same man they used before to hack in. Now the brains behind the operation has him making the demands, so he's not running the show. I intercepted some of the messages last time. This all but proves we're also working against the original mastermind. That's the guy we want, so we have to get junior first."

Tess was impressed in spite of herself. "Fine. Now if we only had a name, we'd be in business."

"Oh, I have that. I'll also know him when I see him. Zahi Selim, an Egyptian ex-patriot. Young, around twenty-five or twenty-six. His family cut him loose when his behavior got too extreme, even for them. His father's in the export business, textiles, and owns a number of European properties in major cities. Sort of like Fayed. You know, the father of Princess Di's boyfriend?"

"The one killed in the crash with her? You mean, this Selim guy we're looking for is a *playboy?*"

"And was working it big-time until Daddy cut him off and he ran out of money. Hopefully he'll be returning to his former habits if he got an advance on this job. I almost had enough on him in London and reported what I had. My superior ordered him arrested without giving me prior notice. I had argued against it, but he didn't listen."

"Ah," Tess said. "And they had to let him go. Not enough proof to hold him. Now he's at it again."

Cochran sighed and relaxed in his seat, tapping his long fingers on the armrests. *Nerves or controlled anger?* "My objections to his arrest were misconstrued."

Tess regarded his expression, a mixture of disgust and resignation. "But you know him by sight? What if he recognizes you?"

"He won't. I tracked him down and kept tabs on him, hoping for rock-solid proof of his involvement, but we never actually met. Mercier said he'd send a photo taken when Selim was in custody in London so you can see what he looks like." Cochran frowned. "He's a ballsy little son of a bitch. I'll give him that. Smart, too, in some ways."

"So how do we approach him?" Tess asked, getting excited now about a quick resolution to the op.

"*We* don't. *You* do. He's a sucker for fast women. Rich women willing to finance his habit. I want you to befriend him and entice him to come on board the yacht for a ride up the coast, supposedly to Monaco, where you two can gamble. Maybe offer him a little private action on the way."

"Seems like a lot of trouble. Why don't we just grab him? That would be simpler, wouldn't it?"

"Risky. If he put up a fight, our grab might be misconstrued as an assault, or worse. If we render him unconscious, how would that look at the marina?"

"We could take him to the airport and back on the jet," she suggested.

He shrugged. "Same thing. How would we get him out on the tarmac and onto the plane without being observed? I don't know about you, but I don't think I want an arrest for kidnapping added to my less than stellar record. Mercier could straighten it out eventually, I know, but our boy would be out of our hands for the duration. Better if he comes along willingly."

"I see your point," she agreed.

"Fine. We'll need to get the location of his computer first. You'll get him to take you home with him if you can, and you'll pinpoint where it is. Then we'll have located our proof. Next, once you've enticed him onto the yacht and we're out to sea, we'll get some answers." He looked over at her with a smile. "Then maybe I'll dump the little bastard overboard and see how the sharks like garbage."

Tess smiled and shook her head. "You'd never do *that.*"

"Don't think so?" He looked entirely too serious.

"Would you?"

He shrugged. "Depends on how cooperative he is and how I feel at the time."

"Stop yanking my chain, Cochran. You're treating me like a trainee agent, and I'm definitely not that. I've been around the block a time or two."

"Fine, so take your hair down, show a little cleavage and let's see your sexy look."

Tess jerked upright in her seat and glared. *"What?"*

"So I can see if you have what it takes to persuade our boy to ride the seas with you. Looks like you might need a little work."

"Go straight to hell!" she gasped, clutching her chest with one hand and the armrest with the other.

He closed his eyes and blew out a deep breath. "Well. A *lotta* work."

Tess had never wanted to slap a man so badly before in her life. Instead, she stood up and marched to the back of the plane, into the bathroom, and slammed the door.

She leaned against the tiny sink and tried to calm down. When she could breathe normally, she raised her eyes to look in the mirror, attempting to assess her features objectively.

Could she entice with these looks? Would any man in his right mind follow her onto a boat?

Not unless she stole his wallet. Cochran was right. She needed a *lotta* work.

She let down her hair and fluffed it, letting a slightly wavy lock fall over one eye. Sexy? Maybe a little if she ditched the outfit and went back in there stark naked. Or maybe not.

Cochran was seriously impacting her self-image. Her image frowned back at her.

"I can *do* this!" she said in a desperate whisper.

Half an hour later she pranced back into the main cabin, copying the exaggerated runway strut of models she'd seen on television, and posed, hand on her hip, to get his reaction.

His lips pursed and his left eyebrow quirked up as he looked her over. His gaze traveled over her like a laser, burning her confidence to ashes as it tracked from her hair, over her skimpiest, half-buttoned sweater, over her straight-leg Kleins, right down to her strappy little sandals and back again. Then he looked away without so much as a comment.

What *was* he thinking?

"Well?" she demanded, resting both hands on her hips.

He smiled up at her. "The look is adequate, but I think the attitude will have to change. Sit down."

She plopped into the seat across the aisle from him and crossed her arms over her chest. "Face it. I'm no femme fatale. Not in my genes."

"Hey, the jeans are great. Could be a little tighter, but the cut is right and the color's good. The sweater's way too cutesy, though, even left open like that. And you'll need a push-up."

"Bra? You're telling me what kind of *bra* to wear?" Tess was incensed. And red. She could feel her face burning. "So I'm a thirty-four B. Sue me!"

"Look," he began with a studied blink and a sigh that

screamed impatience. "Don't take this personally. I'm trying to be helpful here. Sexy is in the attitude, and yours is too…uptight."

She rolled her eyes and threw up her hands. "As opposed to down and *loose?*"

He grinned and nodded. "Finally the *aha!* moment. See, you're halfway there, just knowing that. Now all you have to do is loosen up."

Loosen up? Damn, if he said that again, she'd smack him!

She jumped up, paced down the aisle, turned and paced back, fists clenched. He made her feel like a weird old prude with ice water in her veins! And she wasn't! She was *not!*

Furious beyond words, Tess leaned over, grabbed his face with both hands and kissed him soundly on the mouth. She could be sexy. She'd show him just how sexy she could be when she put her mind to it.

But her mind strayed dangerously when her lips met his, and her fury was the last thing on it.

Chapter 3

Cameron almost jumped back in shock, but the feel and taste of her lips registered quickly enough to prevent that. Instead, he leaned into the kiss and deepened it immediately.

Damn, the girl must have been around the block to kiss this way. He grasped her waist, pulled her down on his lap and let the good times roll.

He had kissed a lot of women, but even in her anger, this one had a sweetness, a freshness and an eagerness he had seldom enjoyed. Yeah, he could work with her, with this. *Man, oh, man.*

As suddenly as that she jerked her head back and stared at him, wide-eyed. With shock?

"Hey, *you* kissed *me*," he reminded her, adding a quizzical smile to put her at ease.

She jumped off his lap as if he'd bitten her. "Well, it won't happen again!" she announced as she backed into the seat across the aisle and sat down with a plop. "That was just…just to…well, *show* you."

"Well, you sure got my attention, I'll give you that." He crossed his legs to hide his erection. If the kiss had scared her that much, he didn't want her to run and lock herself in the back cabin.

"I *can* be sexy," she declared, crossing her arms over her chest and slinging one jeans-clad leg over the other.

Cameron nodded. "Yes, you can. I'm convinced."

"Don't you patronize me! I hate it when men patronize me," she snapped.

Damn. "Okay, make me some ground rules here. I'm just a guy, and we pretty much take things at face value unless we're told otherwise. So, you can kiss me, but I can't kiss you back?"

"Exactly," she said with a firm nod, still keeping her eyes averted. Then she shook her head. "No. There won't be any more kissing. Understand? No kissing. At all."

"Okay, got it. Then I'm guessing sex is out of the question?"

"This is not funny!"

He shook his head. "And I'm not laughing. Not one giggle. Any more rules I should know about?" He thought he heard her laugh, looked over and saw that she was shaking with laughter, biting her lips shut and shaking. "Oh, so you can laugh, but I can't. Okay, I'll write that down."

"Shut *up!*" she said, letting go and laughing out loud.

"This is so absurd. I honestly don't know why I kissed you. I apologize."

"As well you should," he said, straight-faced. "I hate being harassed, and you should know better."

Her laugh calmed to a smile, an apologetic one. "I shouldn't have reacted to your merely pointing out the obvious. I'm just a little sensitive about my shortcomings. From now on, I promise to take whatever advice you have for me."

"Shortcomings?" he asked, seeing that, despite the smile, she was dead serious about how she saw herself. "Not being a sexpot is no shortcoming, Tess. Mind if I call you Tess?"

"No, but I thought…"

"None of what I said was intended as criticism. You have a natural appeal that's fantastic."

She blushed again. "Thanks for saying that, but—"

"But we need blatant, in-your-face sexy, though, to hook this guy, because that's the type he goes for."

She looked thoughtful. "And if I can manage that?"

Good. She was on board, being reasonable. "As I said, I want you to find out where he's based so we can retrieve his computers for evidence later. Flatter him. Get him to show you where he lives. Or maybe just tell you where he lives. In either case, do whatever you need to do to have him go with you on the boat."

"Whatever I need to do? I'm *not* having sex with him," she declared. "That's out of the question."

"No," he agreed, "but you can sort of promise it if that's what it takes." Cameron watched her frown. "Can't you?"

She nodded but shifted uncomfortably in her seat,

arms crossed over her breasts, an attitude of self-protection. "I guess so."

"Nobody expects the ultimate sacrifice, Tess," he assured her. "I'll be close by. If he gets too frisky for comfort, you can always deck him and we'll go to Plan B."

She granted him a sidewise glare. "But it would be better if I simply wriggled away and played it coy."

"Exactly. Undercover work requires acting ability. Just consider this a role," he suggested.

She shook her head. "If this is what it takes, why on earth didn't Mercier send one of the others? *Look* at me!" She gave herself an impatient wave and sighed.

Cameron knew instinctively that flattery wouldn't work with Tess. She would see right through that, so he opted for honesty. "I'm sure he sent you because you're a solid, no-nonsense agent with good credentials and he figured you'd get the job done."

She scoffed. "Little did he know…"

Cameron smiled. "Hey, you got me on board, so he was right about that. The next part is to catch the guy, and we'll do that, too. However, the method of apprehending him is all *my* idea, not Mercier's. I do believe it will work, Tess. I know you can do it."

"Wish I had your confidence," she replied, but he could see she was a little more willing, considering it possible. She lifted her hands in a small gesture of resignation. "Okay, so I'll give it my best shot, whatever that's worth." She relaxed a little, uncrossed her arms and turned sideways in her seat to face him. "So, fake promise, push-up bra, flashier clothes. What else?"

"Killer heels. A little bling. Clingy dress. Heavy on the makeup. We'll practice your expressions after the makeover."

"Sleepy eyes, pouty lips, shoulders back, chest out," she mused, deepening her voice to a throaty growl.

Cameron grinned when she made an exaggerated pout. "By jove, I think she's got it!"

"Henry Higgins, you ain't," she said with a roll of her eyes and a snort.

Good. She was loosening up at last, giving him a little trust, acknowledging that he had experience in adopting a fake persona to get a job done. Maybe he was underestimating her ability to adapt. "You'll be great," he promised.

"And just what will you be doing during my great performance?"

"Bodyguarding. No beautiful, wealthy woman in her right mind would go trolling in Saint-Tropez without protection. You'll convince him I'm only a hireling. Soon as you get him on board, I'll hop on to captain your little yacht while you two party. You keep him busy drinking, gambling or whatever while I take us well down the coast. Then we pounce, get the info we need and that's that."

"Then what do we do with him?" she asked as she got up and went forward to the small fridge. "And don't say 'Toss him over the side.'" She returned with two sodas and handed him one.

"I'll arrange with your boss to have someone meet us at sea and transport him back to the States. You and I will return to Saint-Tropez, or wherever he's based, and collect his computer and whatever other evidence we find." He popped the top on his can and offered her a toast. "Here's to a faultless bust."

She clinked his can with hers. "Without incident."

They fell silent then, each lost in thought. Cameron felt they had a pretty good shot at nabbing this guy and at least delaying the threatened blackout. But what about the stateside conspirator, undoubtedly the brains of the enterprise? If the pip-squeak didn't give him up, they'd still have the problem, probably sooner than later.

He cast a look over at Tess and saw her worried expression. Was she thinking the same thing, or were her concerns still centered on her ability to seduce? He remembered the kiss and smiled. She had it in her, all right.

Cameron stood and looked down at her. "Hey, you're not beating yourself up over kissing me, are you?"

She glanced up and shrugged. "Yes, well, I am sorry about that. Really."

He leaned down and caught her lips with his, his hand clasping her neck as he deepened the kiss. Then, reluctantly, he released her. "There. Now we're even."

Tess kept stealing looks at him that next hour. After blowing her mind with that kiss, he had calmly walked up front and rifled through the cabinet for something to eat. Obviously it hadn't meant anything. To him, anyway.

To her, it meant she was in serious danger of risking the entire mission. How the devil was she supposed to concentrate on what she was hired to do? The man was a walking sex bomb, causing a buzz in her brain and body that seriously interfered with her thought processes.

Why on earth didn't she react to his touch the way she always had with others? With Brian, she had practically forced herself to respond, to keep from shying away from him. Her ready response to this man actually scared her a little, because it came so naturally.

She watched furtively as he returned to his seat, opened a bag of chips and settled down to work on his computer. *Way too cool. No, make that way too hot,* she thought with a sigh.

It wasn't that she had anything against sex, but she truly believed it ought to mean something other than pure gratification. He was making her want that very thing. She felt no better than all those licentious free-love advocates her mom had described. These impulses were something to fight, not embrace. Especially given what she'd been sent to do.

"You ought to get some sleep," he said as he plinked away on the keys of his laptop and studied the screen.

Yeah, right. Her nerves were tingling like crazy, and her thoughts were all over the place. "I can't sleep. What are you doing?"

"Reviewing the case notes I saved."

"Weren't they classified?" she asked.

"They're not the official report, just my personal observations. You might want to read through these before you meet him."

"If you need to go online, my laptop is on satellite."

"Mine, too, but thanks," he said, still not looking at her. "We're flying into Nice, right?"

"That's the plan."

"I wonder why he's based in Tropez, where there's

not much action. Not in the way of gambling, anyway. Nice or Monaco, where the big casinos are, would make more sense."

She shrugged. "Maybe he's kicked his habit. It's been a couple of years."

"He would need money for it and probably got an advance on this job. Let's hope so, anyway. He'll be easier to find if he's still gambling."

"So you don't think his motive is political?"

Cameron smiled and shook his head. "Not a chance. Gaming is his first love, testing his smarts. Maybe he's an addict, maybe not, but he loves it. He wouldn't do it online, at least not exclusively, because he also loves the casino scene and the flashy women he meets there. All that takes money, a lot of it."

"And he knew where to get it."

"That's why he's in this, then and now. You can bet he has a state-of-the-art computer set up somewhere to play with. The hacking is also a game to him, and he thrives on games."

She toyed with a strand of her hair, twisting it around her finger. "With women, too, you think?"

"Of course. He likes to believe he's God's gift to the female gender, handsome, charming and clever as all get out."

"Is he?" she asked with a worried little frown.

"Pretty much. You'll see. So don't underestimate him."

"Did you?" She actually smiled, a not-so-subtle taunt.

Cameron shrugged. "Maybe, but I'd have had him if I could have gone in alone and caught him before he erased the evidence. He was fast, I'll give him that. Less than three minutes' warning as they busted down his door. Before they got to him, his computers were clean as a school library system."

"They thought you warned him?"

"Yes, well, to be fair, sometimes operatives *do* get sympathetic feelings for the subjects when they delve that deeply into their lives and see the reasons behind the behavior."

"You like this guy?" Her look accused.

"I know him. I get why he does it. He's young, kind of clueless in some respects, and I think he was used, but no, I don't like him." Cameron sighed. "He's a spoiled, selfish brat who resents anyone in authority, and he believes he's a genius."

"So you don't think he's a hardened terrorist out to destroy a country."

"Not my call. I reel 'em in. Somebody else guts them."

She sighed and sat back, patting the armrests with her palms. "Well, he's a pretty big fish, and I'm not familiar with the fishing gear."

"Don't worry. I'm the gear. You're the bait." Cameron smiled at the analogy. "Trust me, sweetie, you'll be the juciest worm on the hook."

She let it go at that and began studying the notes on his computer. Cameron busied himself working out the details of transforming her. He looked forward to seeing her reactions and instructing her in what to do. She was a lot less predictable than he'd first imagined. His thoughts kept returning to her kiss. And his.

If they ever got to the point of equal involvement, he wondered what would happen next. He knew it would lead to sex if she let it, but what then? It had been a long time since he'd been interested in *what then*.

The girl was unique, not his type and definitely out of bounds. He knew he'd better keep things on a professional level. There was too much at stake not to do that. A little slap and tickle between temporary partners wasn't all that unusual, but it was typically only stress relief or just plain fun. Tess was so far above that, he couldn't even imagine her approving, much less participating. It would have to mean something a whole lot deeper, and he didn't do deeper. Not after that struggle getting over Brenda.

Resignation replaced his anticipation. Business only, then. No more kissing, one-sided or not. That sure lent a boatload of urgency to the mission. He'd do what he needed to do, get it over with and go home. Forget her and the job. Fish. Drink beer. Shoot the breeze at the bar and fish some more.

Maybe he ought to get to know her better, though. It only made sense to get a firm grasp on who he was working with and how she thought. Right?

He did understand her enough to know she'd expect tit for tat, so he turned to her. "Since we've teamed up for this, do you have any questions about me you'd like to ask?"

"Like what?" She looked wary.

"Oh, I dunno." Cameron leaned on the armrest and cocked his head to one side. "Personal stuff. For instance, how did you get into this business, anyway?"

She smiled. "Okay, how did you get into this business, anyway?"

"Majored in international studies and minored in

criminal justice at Georgia. Joined the army and did three years. When I got out, Savannah seemed too small town. I applied to the Company and moved to D.C. How about you? I heard that those special teams are formed by invitation only."

She looked thoughtful. "They are. I was recruited."

"Because you had some kind of special talent? I heard that each of your agents is required to have something unique, an edge that would be useful in counter-intelligence beyond the obvious skills required."

"You heard all that, did you?" Her smile was provocative.

"You know how the intel grapevine works. The CIA had a big study going on for years that involved paranormal activities. Rumor has it that didn't stop when the funding did. So what's your trick?"

Her gaze met his, and she said nothing for a full minute. Then she answered. "I read people fairly well, that's all."

"Minds, that sort of thing?" he asked, pressing her.

"Mostly I pick up visual clues, expressions, body language and so forth."

"Fascinating. How did you study for that?"

She frowned and looked away. "That's getting really personal."

"Hey, working together as closely as we will is personal. Trust is necessary. It pays to know your partner as well as you can."

"I suppose you have a point. As long as you reciprocate, I guess it won't matter. After all, we'll probably never even see one another when the mission's over.

Unless you go to work for us." She had leaned back against the headrest and spoke as if she were talking to herself. "And if you do, we'll need to be…acquainted. All right then."

Cameron realized how hard it must be for her to share information about herself, but she was doing it, anyway, because she thought he was right.

Her voice was totally unemotional. "During my early childhood, I began to acquire the knack for it, mostly out of self-preservation. When my mom crossed her arms over her chest and her lips tightened so much they almost disappeared and her eyes narrowed, that meant Dad had it coming. When he'd pace like a caged tiger, stopping only to throw back his head and grit his teeth, I ran to hide."

"They were abusive?" he asked, guessing.

"Oh, no, not at all. My parents never struck me or unleashed their anger directly at me, but I watched their arguments from a place of safety. Under the dining-room table was my favorite place. Anyway, that was the beginning of my fascination with physical clues to what people were thinking and planning to do."

Cameron sighed. "I guess we take inspiration wherever we find it."

She offered a little lopsided smile to that but still didn't look at him as she continued. "Later, when I could choose my own books from the library, I studied everything I could find on the subject. Nuances of behavior became things to watch for. So did breathing patterns and variations in facial muscles. By the time I reached high school, I was convinced I'd become an expert."

"Had all those teachers pegged, did you?"

"Absolutely. Excelled on the debate team, too. Knew when I had 'em on the run. I began to concentrate on eyes in particular and grew amazed at what you could glean from a person's actual thoughts, some as clear as if they spoke them out loud."

He felt a little uneasy. Could she read his thoughts? "Can you read me?" he asked, trying to keep his voice light and conversational, afraid she wouldn't answer truthfully.

She shook her head. "No, so don't worry. *Some* is the key word. Very few, in fact, and then only some of the time."

"I see. Well, every little bit helps on the job, I bet."

"You're up," she said, turning her head to look at him. "And I am a very good lie detector when I switch it on."

"I'm guessing you just did. What would you like to know?"

"Your parents, are they deceased?"

He laughed and sat back, aping her former position and looking straight ahead at the back of the seat in front of him. "Nope. They're still kicking around Savannah. Don't see much of them, though. They weren't too thrilled with my choice of occupations. Dad wanted me to go into business with him. Mom wanted me to marry and settle down on the next block and give her grandbabies."

"No wife, no kids, no siblings," she said. And she knew that because she'd read his record. He wished he had the same advantage.

"Just me, the black sheep who strayed from the fold

and is too proud to listen to any more 'I told you sos' than I have to. Our family get-togethers are usually brief and real predictable."

"Same here. My mom and dad grew up in an isolated commune left over from the seventies. Genuine California hippies, protests, free love, drugs, you name it. They ran away from that, all the way across the country, when they were seventeen and expecting me. They thought they'd invented monogamy."

"Joined the good ol' establishment, huh?"

She huffed a wry little laugh. "Not exactly. They didn't know *how.* I give them an A for effort, though. They had trouble holding down jobs for any length of time but they stayed off dope and were faithful to each other, as far as I know. Home schooling in the commune was hit or miss, so they said, but they did manage to get their GEDs and Dad went to trade school."

"That's remarkable, don't you think?"

"They certainly are remarkable, all right. Don't know if that's good or bad."

"What do they do now?" he asked, astounded that she had opened up to him this way and fearing he'd have to keep doing the same. She had a way about her that made it too easy to share, and before he knew it, she'd learn more about him than anybody else in the world knew.

He felt he'd already told her more than he was comfortable with. But the more he learned about Tess's life, the more he wanted to know.

"Dad's an electrician, and Mom works for a florist."

"I bet they're proud of you," Cameron said, feeling

proud of her himself for all she had accomplished. He knew she had to have put herself through college.

"I don't know if they are or not. They don't get what I'm all about, that's for sure. My mom calls me a changeling."

"Stranger in the nest. I guess we have something in common, then. That's good, don't you think?"

"It's a little weird," she said, nodding. "Do you miss what you used to do?"

"I like what I do now. Work for myself. Stress free. Great location," he replied, wondering if she realized he hadn't really answered the question.

She looked at him and smiled knowingly. "Why don't you take a nap, Cochran? You don't want to talk anymore."

Good guess. That's what that was. Or maybe she was adept at mind reading. There were those rumors about the SEXTANT and COMPASS teams. He'd have to watch himself if he didn't want her to *really* know him.

Chapter 4

Cameron followed Tess's lead as they retrieved their bags from the back of the plane and made their way down to the tarmac. He stopped for a moment and drew in a deep draught of the night air after leaving the stuffiness of the plane's cabin.

He loved the Riviera. Everything was close to the water, and every town, burg and beach was usually teeming with people there to have a good time. The entire coastline had a laid-back party atmosphere.

The level of sophistication was like no other, though a great deal of it was pretense. Everybody liked to think they were rich whether they were or not, and this was certainly a prime place to do that. He found the people watching great entertainment.

They hopped a shuttle to the main terminal and

whisked through customs, belongings intact, as soon as they identified themselves. Mercier had cleared the way.

"We'll get started in the morning, when the shops open," he said as he headed for the bank on the upper level to exchange their funds for euros.

"I hope we'll be able to get a car at this hour," she said as he waited for the exchange to be completed.

"We'll taxi. It's not far to the marina. We'll shop in the morning, then sail on down to Saint-Tropez."

He noted how she paled at the mention of sailing. This could be a problem, he realized. He didn't relish the idea of her barfing every few minutes and being miserable the whole time. Maybe he could fix that.

In short order, they were on their way to the marina and the *Jezebel,* a sixty-footer with a fifteen foot beam and a top speed of thirty-two knots. Mercier had promised it was air-conditioned and roomy enough to impress. Cameron got excited just thinking about it and couldn't wait to board her.

The marina was lit up like Times Square at Christmas, he noticed as the taxi dropped them off at the boardwalk. He had to exhibit a little false cool to keep from rushing to slip twenty-two.

Tess was busy gaping at the surrounding scenery while he was zeroed in on the boats. And there she was! He stopped just to take her in. She was long and lean as a spearhead honed out of white granite. "What a beauty!" he exclaimed in an almost reverent whisper.

"What did you say? What? The boat? Which one is it?" Tess asked.

"Which one is *she?*" he corrected. "There she is," he said, pointing. "Just look at her!"

"Humph. You sound like you're in love, Cochran. It's only a boat."

"But what a boat! Man, I'd give my eyeteeth to own her. C'mon, let's go." He didn't wait. Couldn't.

He lifted his bag and Tess's over the rail and stepped onto the aft deck, loving the feel of it beneath his feet. He went up to check the fuel level first, then viewed the controls to make certain the boat was adequate for their needs. "Who am I kidding?" he asked himself. "This baby has everything. State of the art."

"Good grief. You sound like a kid who just got his first bike," she said. When he turned, he saw her exploring the saloon.

"Look at this. It even has a bar. This is a party boat," she announced, bouncing down on the cushy banquette seat, then leaning back. "Comfy enough for royalty."

The seating was set diagonally in a reversed S-form curved around a table at one end. The bar looked well stocked.

"Let's see the cabins," he suggested, walking toward the bow, where he knew the smaller of the two would be. The forward cabin was nearly wall-to-wall berth, but beautifully outfitted. He knew the master cabin would dwarf it. "I'll take this one. You'll need room to entertain."

"Get real. That man will never see my bed," she promised.

Cameron laughed. "Go check it out. Will you let *me* see it?"

She marched aft and opened the door to the master

cabin. "Okay, you can look. I know you've fallen head over heels for this tub and want the full tour."

When she stepped back to let him pass, his chest brushed hers. For a moment, he stopped and had eyes only for the woman who was bravely facing what was probably her worst nightmare.

Only then did he realize how clipped her words had been and how stiffly she walked. He had forgotten her fear in his delirium over the most expensive vessel he'd ever been aboard, much less captained.

"Are you okay?" he asked. "We're sitting still in the water, you know. The waves are barely lapping tonight, but you look a little green around the gills."

"I'm perfectly fine," she declared and moved away from him. "Where…where's the bathroom?"

"The head," he said, correcting her automatically. "In there."

She ran, hand over her mouth. *Well, damn.* Cameron went topside, as much to give her privacy to be sick as to check out what other wonders the *Jezebel* possessed. He admitted he was in awe. Not too cool of him, but he couldn't help it.

When Tess had plenty of time to recover and still hadn't joined him, he went back below deck to see about her. She was sound asleep, curled in the middle of the king-size berth in her cabin. He gently closed the door and went back to admiring their new digs. Morning would arrive in a few hours, and he had slept a little on the plane.

Right now he wanted to familiarize himself with the controls and marvel over everything. Tess was right. He had fallen in love. He liked that she understood his passion, even if she did think it was ridiculous. He wondered if she had a passion herself and what that might be.

By the time the sun was up, gilding the Côte d'Azur, he found he was thinking more about Tess's attributes than those of the *Jezebel*. Not a good sign.

"Up and at 'em, Miz Bradshaw! We're doing the girl thing this morning and shopping till we drop!"

He saw she was right where he'd left her, still dressed and in the same position. "You alive?" he asked, reaching down to shake one of her feet. She had great legs. He let go of her quickly, before it seemed like a caress.

She groaned and pushed up on one elbow. "Are there any sodas in the bar?"

"Coffee's made," he said. "But if you want something cold, name your poison."

"Ginger ale," she said, sliding off the bed. "I'll be out in a minute."

She was as good as her word, appearing on unsteady legs and plopping down on the banquette cushions. "I'm better," she assured him. "I'll get used to it."

"Here. Drink this and don't look out the windows. Forget you're on the water."

"Ha!" She grunted and kept her eyes on her drink. "So, what's the plan for today? We go to Saint-Tropez after we buy me a dress?"

"Buy you a dress and shoes, get you a tan and have your hair and makeup done."

"I hope my expense account can stand all that," she grumbled.

"Spare no expense. That's what the man said."

"Jack said that? Is he nuts? This boat must be costing a fortune, and our funding can't be that generous."

Cameron loved her practical nature, but she simply didn't get it. "The yacht's a repo now owned by the French government and on loan to us as a courtesy. As for your expensive do-over, we have to get this guy on board willingly whatever the cost. You can see how my carrying him aboard unconscious would look. We'd never get out of the bay without somebody reporting it."

"So I'll get him on board," she said dully, sipping her ginger ale slowly and rubbing the cold can against the side of her face.

"I told Mercier we'd zip down the coast of Spain and out into open waters. After that, I figure a maximum of sixteen hours to Conda Isle, where Mercier will have someone waiting to take charge of the prisoner and fly him back to the States."

"Sixteen *hours?*" she exclaimed, wide-eyed. "On open water?"

He sat down beside her and took her hand. "Tess. You can do this. I'll help you. We'll get some tranquilizers, and after we interrogate Selim, I'll lock him up and you can sleep the entire trip if you want to."

She sighed and let her head fall back on the cushion behind her. "Kill me now."

"Forget the boat for now. Let's go into town and buy you something pretty. Think how much fun you'll have undercover."

"I'm not in this for the fun of it," she stated. "And you shouldn't be, either."

"There's nothing wrong with enjoying what you do for a living. Trust me, it's the best time you can have standing up."

Not really, but he needed to distract her, and the truth wouldn't do it.

"I have to shower and change," she said, her voice sounding awfully weak.

Yeah, he'd just been thinking that standing up in the shower with him would be the best time. However, that was not an appropriate thought, and not one to be shared out loud.

Cameron stood and tugged her upright. Her hair was a mess, her skin pale as milk, and her clothes were full of creases. She looked tumbled and lovely. And pretty damned hot. "Don't bother changing. You're fine just the way you are."

She must have been desperate to get off the boat, because she went with him, just as she was.

Tess wished she'd had another hour's sleep, and time to shampoo her hair, shower and change, but she had so needed to get her feet on solid land. This op was going to prove a lot harder than she'd imagined.

"I don't even take my trash out looking like this," she muttered as they strode along the quay.

He smiled down at her. "You look cute a little rumpled. Don't worry about it. I promise you, we won't see a soul you know."

"I'm not really vain," she explained, sticking her hands in the pockets of her jeans. "It's just that I feel so much better facing the world behind a little makeup.

Most women do, you know. Being a guy, you wouldn't understand."

"Oh, I get it," he stated. He was silent for a moment, then added, "Really. You've heard that adage 'Clothes make the man'? Well, clothes can make the woman, too. Not in the sense it was probably said in the first place, but the way you're decked out really can change your whole attitude, how you walk, how you talk, how you interact with other people. Since you're a body-language expert, I tell you this for future reference. You can take on a new persona and pretend much more easily to be someone you're not when you're dressed for it. You'll see."

"Thanks for the info. You've done a lot of undercover work, I take it."

He sighed, shook his head and gave a wry little chuckle. "So much that I sometimes wondered who I really was."

"Ah, but you found your true self on a fishing boat." She lengthened her strides to keep up with him and shot him a half smile. "You looked pretty immersed in the role when I found you, anyway."

"Bloom where you're planted, I always say."

That made her wonder if that, too, was only a role he'd assumed. Maybe he hadn't had much choice. The Company had banned him from any kind of law en-forcement work. Not by any formal directive, but with that shadow on his record, he wouldn't have been able to get a job in a two-man police station.

She recalled the photo of him in his file. Sharp dresser, clean-cut and as professional looking as any agent she knew. So he had done an about-face.

That made a strange sort of sense when she thought about it. Cameron had cut all ties and made a complete change.

They walked in silence for a while. She took in the beauty of the place, with its tall, gently swaying palms and carefully landscaped terrain. The sea air was salty, fresh and bracing, banishing her jet lag by degrees. By the time they reached the shops, she felt rejuvenated.

"You wouldn't be female if you didn't look forward to this a little bit," he said, his tone teasing. "Confess now. You can't wait, can you?"

"All right, maybe a little anticipation," she said. Trepidation, too, however. What if she couldn't pull it off?

No woman appreciated being told she was dowdy, even if she was and liked it. Well, he hadn't said that exactly, but he'd probably thought it.

Now he looked like a million bucks. Like he had a million, anyway.

There was the two-day growth of beard, which some thought looked so cool. His hair was sun streaked and in casual disarray, which stylists worked so hard to arrange. His nails were neatly trimmed and buffed. The diamond stud in his left ear added a rakish touch.

He carried himself with such confidence, she envied it. Hers was sorely lacking at the moment, but she could act as if it wasn't. Surely she had that much acting ability.

They soon reached the main shopping area of Nice. Classy shops, famous brand names, tourists and locals spending big. Tess tried to look cool and not stare.

"There," he said, pointing to a salon with a tasteful

swirl that spelled out *Paolo*. "That's the place. Now then, you're my project. Go along with whatever I say, and don't look surprised."

"Nothing you do would surprise me at this point," she said testily.

But she found she was wrong. He swept the door open and ushered her inside with a gushing spate of Italian. She had no idea what he was saying, because she didn't speak the language. Since this was actually the French Riviera, he must have taken his cue from the name of the place. Maybe he'd chosen it because of that.

She looked up at him and nodded, which seemed to be what he wanted her to do. His wide smile of approval and one-armed hug said so, anyway.

The place was amazing. Tess had never indulged in a spa/salon. The entry was done in muted silver with swaths of bright gold lettering on the walls and a fountain with a gold-leafed statue of a nude pouring water into the shell that surrounded her feet.

Cameron greeted the pretty receptionist in Italian, flirting outrageously. Tess didn't need to understand the words to get that. The girl gave as good as she got, too, before punching an intercom with an inch-long silver fingernail and announcing them.

Seconds later a young man with long, silky hair and a deep tan appeared. Was he wearing mascara? Cameron greeted him like an old friend and introduced Tess, almost as an afterthought.

Then the young man spoke to her in English with a heavy Italian accent. "Come, Giacomo is to make you beautiful. Mama will not know you when he has finished!"

"Your mama or mine?" she muttered drily, aping his accent.

"Smile, my sweet girl. I geev you the chance to change your world!"

"Oh, thank you, *Fabio,*" she replied under her breath.

She saw him stifle a laugh, but he kept up the act.

Giacomo the Pretty showed her to a room, where a female assistant indicated she should undress. Curious about what would happen next, Tess followed instructions. Then she was immersed in mud, washed, massaged, steamed, spray tanned and air-dried.

Cloaked in a warm terry robe, she followed the assistant to another private room where she was manicured and pedicured, polished, shampooed and conditioned.

When she rejoined Cameron and Giacomo, old pals for sure now, Cameron eagerly asked her how she felt after her treatment.

"Like I've been through an automatic car wash," she replied sweetly.

He laughed uproariously, as did Giacomo, though she doubted the little Italian had understood a word she'd said. Giacomo motioned her to the chair in front of the mirror, and she took a seat.

Cameron looked on anxiously, offering suggestions as Giacomo combed out her hair, trimmed it and brushed in highlights, which he wrapped in foil.

"Now I'm an alien," she commented, rolling her eyes at the sight in the mirror. "And I thought I looked bad when I came in here."

They paid no attention to anything she said. She became an object to decorate, and the two of them had a high old time arguing, gesturing wildly and apparently compromising as Giacomo worked his magic.

He had swiveled her chair after he'd twisted her hair into rolls. She wouldn't be able to see what they did to her next.

Then another guy arrived, long faced and thin, already assessing her as his new project. Tess stared back pointedly, asserting herself, but he didn't seem to get or perhaps didn't care that she was copying his expression.

Giacomo almost bowed to the man, while Cameron treated him with great deference. No arguing with this artist. He had game.

She abandoned herself to the long-fingered hands with the featherlight touch and hoped to heck he knew what he was doing. At any rate, if he didn't, she could always wash her face.

"Voilà!" he said finally, a pleased exclamation. So maybe that was why Cameron and Giacomo hadn't put in their two cents' worth. He must be French.

"Merci," she ventured.

As if just realizing she was a real person, not a mannequin, he smiled at her, tapped her once under the chin and left.

Giacomo went to work with his blow-dryer and fingers, lost in the act of creating her new hairstyle. She felt him pin up loops and spring down curls.

Her excitement grew in spite of her will to remain aloof. So did the gut-wrenching concern. What if no amount of disguising her could make her sexy enough to entice the man they were after? And even if they gave her the looks, could she act well enough to pull it off?

The whole mission could hinge on it.

Chapter 5

At length, the little stylist stood back from Tess and held his hands out, signaling that he had finished his creation. She watched him and Cameron exchange a look. Both nodded and smiled.

Then Cameron stepped behind her chair, dragged the robe off her shoulders, baring them and half her breasts. She grabbed it for modesty's sake as he turned her around.

When she looked up, a stranger in the mirror stared back. "My God!"

"Bellissima!" Cameron said in a reverent whisper.

"Si!" Giacomo beamed at her reflection.

Cameron continued to stare for a moment, then spoke quietly to Giacomo. In the mirror, she thought she saw money change hands behind her.

Moments later she and Cameron were alone. "What

do you think?" he asked, his look now assessing, rather than admiring. The man changed moods on a dime.

She shrugged. "You were absolutely right. I'm somebody else now."

"Not quite, but you're getting there. Go get dressed. We aren't through yet."

The jeans and top she had worn looked ridiculous with her new look, as if she'd put a different head on her body. She vaguely recalled doing that with her Barbie dolls years ago. It had seemed simpler than changing their clothes.

An hour later they exited the second shop with a too short, formfitting, low-cut cocktail dress in electric blue. It seemed to have been constructed for the new underwear they had purchased for her at the first store. Thank goodness, he hadn't insisted on fitting her push-up bra!

He directed her into a shoe shop and immediately chose killer high-heeled sandals that were transparent. "You have beautiful feet. And these will make your legs look longer, giving you height."

"I'll be four inches taller, and that's a fact." She hated them. "Crippled, maybe, but taller. I'm sure a man who hates women designed these."

"You're probably right about that." He shook his head in wonder. "It always amazes me how much women will suffer to look great."

"Hey, this was your idea! All of it! I was perfectly satisfied to look the way I did before, and now you're blaming *me* for having stuff *you* picked out?"

He hailed a taxi. "You'll be perfect for the part you need to play if you'll just smile and quit fighting it.

Attitude is everything and can make or kill a disguise. We'll work on that this afternoon."

He opened the taxi's door and stood back for her to get in. "Careful with your hairdo, and don't mess it up."

Tess wanted to slug him. His adoring look in the mirror had been so damn fake. He didn't like her this way. He didn't like her before. What the hell did she care whether he liked her or not? But she did, against all reason. All of this was just too confusing.

What she needed to do was forget his opinions altogether and concentrate on the mission at hand, on becoming someone who would intrigue a man she didn't even know yet. It would be nice if she knew where her charm switch was.

"Tess?" Cameron's voice was soft, and she turned to look at him. "Don't worry that this will change who you really are. Like I said, just think of yourself as an actress in a role. When the play's over, you can be Tess again, exactly as you were."

She wondered if she would. Or if she even wanted to. "The roles you played changed you, didn't they?"

He inclined his head, as if thinking about that. "Well, on a few ops I got too immersed for too long. Sometimes it was fun and games, like today at the salon. Other times, not so much."

"Yeah, that wasn't even necessary, the byplay with Giacomo and the girl at the desk. What was with that?"

He smiled. "Just practice. Showing off a little for you, I guess."

"Who are you really, Cameron?" she asked, genuinely interested.

"Just a guy trying to get by, mostly."

"A loner."

He nodded.

She wondered if that was by choice or the result of what had happened on his last mission. Choice, most likely, since he'd been an operative for years before his fall from grace. Certainly a loner, then.

"Me, too. Always have been," she admitted. "You need to show me how to be a convincing extrovert. It won't come naturally, but I'll give it all I've got."

"That's the spirit," he said with little enthusiasm. "But first, I have to get you over the motion sickness."

Oh, Lord, she had forgotten they had to go back to the boat! "How do you plan to do that?"

"Hypnosis."

"Oh, no!" she said, shaking her head so vehemently, a curl tumbled out of its pinning. Let him probe her brain and dig out all the secrets of her life? "That's been tried. I can't be hypnotized."

"Okay."

She didn't like that smile he was wearing, one that said he was really looking forward to the treatment and would try it, anyway. Not a chance in hell.

"Let's have lunch before we go back, since we skipped breakfast," he suggested. "I'm starving."

Sweet relief. She would do just about anything to delay getting back on the boat. She didn't even offer a token objection when he had the taxi stop and let them out.

"I know a great place," he said. "You like Italian? I seem to be on an Italian kick today."

Tess nodded and followed him back down the block

to a small trattoria. They entered, and he greeted the host as if he knew him. Either he had spent a lot of time in Nice and had met a lot of the locals, or he got off on being overly gregarious. He was really good at it, too.

"Do you know him?" she asked after they'd been seated at a small table in the darkest corner.

"No, but he probably thinks so. People are more generous to those they know or who know them. Imagine the thousands of people that locals in a tourist area meet. Impossible to remember them all, right? Like Giacomo. He'd probably swear that we'd had dealings before, and so he gave us the star treatment. I knew to speak Italian because of his name. I gave the impression we shared a sexual orientation because that added to his belief that we'd met before."

"So that wasn't practice, just a game or an attempt to shock me," she said.

"It was practice, but with a purpose. I rarely play games just for fun. Remember that," he advised.

She thought about that while he ordered for them in Italian. It was unlike her to surrender that much control, but he obviously knew the menu, since he hadn't even looked at it. Besides, she was too busy thinking about what he'd just told her to concentrate on the food. *Games.* Was he playing games with her? And if he was, what was his purpose?

"Now then," he said. "If you'll let me, I'd like to offer you a few pointers on how to approach our mark when we locate him." He kept his voice low and confidential even though there were few other people in the restaurant and no one was seated close by or paying them the slightest bit of attention.

Tess found she was eager to listen. She had misjudged him. Cameron was all business, did everything for a reason and knew a heck of a lot more about undercover work than she could have learned at the academy. "Sure. I'm listening," she said, leaning forward, elbows on the table, chin propped on her hands.

"First, your expression. You don't want to dazzle him with that smile immediately, but you shouldn't frown, either. Here's a great exercise for that. Relax your body," he said, copying her position. "Wiggle around until you're perfectly comfortable. Totally relaxed. Let the tension go, consciously, muscle by muscle. Good. Now I want you to think about smelling a rose, a sweet, beautiful pink rose. Let your facial muscles go lax and just breathe in. Ah, that's perfect. Keep doing that." His voice was dreamy with that slow Southern drawl. "Inhale the scent… Count the petals…soft and gently curling…"

Tess thought she actually smelled roses.

He hummed with approval. "Deeper breaths now. Close your eyes and inhale slowly. Release your breath. Again. You're getting it now. Dreamy. The rose opens, and you think only of the dazzling scent, filling your senses, sweet and light. You can't get enough…."

Cameron smiled at the easiness with which she went under. He gave her some posthypnotic suggestions and brought her slowly out of her relaxed state to full awareness. "You'll be wonderful at this," he told her. "Your expression is perfect for a first meeting. Intriguing and promising, but not overzealous. You're a good student, Tess."

She blinked several times and looked around. "You really think so?"

"Know so," he declared and raised a hand to motion to the waiter that it was all right to deliver their food now. He would owe the guy a big tip for delaying until signaled, but it was worth it.

Replete with lasagna and wine, they walked back to the marina with their purchases. Cameron watched with amusement as she stepped onto the deck and began looking around at several large yachts moored nearby. "Wow. They make this one look puny, don't they! I wonder who owns them. Celebrities, I bet."

Cameron inclined his head and followed her line of sight. "That one, *La Libra*, belongs to Preston Mc-Elvoy, one of the Fortune Five Hundred. Read about it somewhere."

"This truly is a beautiful place. I'd love to come here on vacation sometime if I can ever afford it."

"Maybe take a slow cruise along the Côte d'Azur?" he asked lazily.

"That would be great, wouldn't it?" She sounded like a child planning Christmas.

So much for her boat phobia. She hadn't turned that ghastly shade of white she usually did the minute she stepped aboard. His trick was working.

"You'd better call Mercier and see what he has for us. They are monitoring any transmissions and might have a more distinct location by now. Also, we need that photo of Selim so you'll recognize him."

She frowned. "You said there's no action in Saint-Tropez. What if he's right here in Nice?"

Cameron shrugged. "Or Monaco. The thing is, we need his computer, and to do that, we need to know where he actually lives. We'll look for him in Saint-Tropez first. If we don't find him there, we'll try the casinos here and in Monaco. But it's really important we locate that computer."

"After we get him, Jack could arrange to have the computer picked up."

"That could be a problem. Even if he's allowed to order the locals, their primary allegiance will be to the Sûreté. We need to get it ourselves. And you know, it might be better if we have it before we question him." He tried to think of a way to do that.

"I could keep him busy while you retrieve it," she said, looking a little worried.

"We'll see how it goes. Maybe I can think of something else. Anyway, let's go below. You've had enough sun today. That fake tan won't protect you against sunburn."

She held out one arm and smoothed a palm over it. "I've never had one before. Does it wash off?"

"It'll last about a week before it starts to fade noticeably. That should be time enough to do what we came to do." He touched the arm they were observing. "You like it well enough to keep it up?"

She shook her head. "No, but it's fun to see what I look like this way. You like it?"

He shouldn't touch that question with a ten-foot pole, but what the hell. "Not as much as I like your fairness. You have great skin."

She beamed. "Thanks. So do you!" Then the beam dimmed as she realized the compliment had just popped out. "I mean, a tan looks good on you. Natural, you know. Like you earned it."

"The hard way. But it's too hot to cover up when you're out in the sun every day."

She touched his hand. "I hope you use sunscreen."

"Ah, you care! Better watch that, or I might take it personally." He loved to tease her. She blushed so easily, and he hadn't known many women who blushed at anything at all.

He watched her hurry below and go to the fridge for a drink. She liked diet soda, he noted, and wondered whether she had to watch her weight. Judging by the way she had consumed that lasagna, he doubted it.

Watching her move was a treat. Some women calculated every motion they made around a man and affected a studied presentation. Tess's moves were as natural as a child's, sometimes hesitant, often quick and efficient, but always perfectly natural. Cameron loved her lack of pretense, even though it would be a definite drawback to her femme fatale persona. He'd have to work on that, but he wished he didn't have to.

He might have added it to the posthypnotic suggestions he'd given her, but those would be lasting, and he did want her to be Tess again. Only minus her fear of boats.

He hadn't even disturbed her inhibitions. If he had, it might have added to her appeal to Selim. But Cameron liked her modesty and valued her too much the way she really was.

"Why don't you take a nap?" he suggested. "I'll call

Mercier, get what he has for us and check out some things by phone. We'll hit the beaches later and start looking for Selim."

She touched her hair. "What if I mess this up? You warned me not to."

"I'll help you fix it. You have had a big morning and will have a bigger night, so get some rest while you can."

"*Roger!* Isn't that what they say on boats?" she asked with a grin.

"Aye, aye, Captain," he returned.

"So you're appointing me captain?"

"No, I was correcting you. I run this tub, and don't you forget it."

She laughed and tossed her soda can into the trash. "No sense of humor on board, I see." Then she sashayed into the master cabin and closed the door.

Cameron could see that being in disguise had already loosened her up a little. Professionally, he was glad. Personally? Well, if he was honest about it, he didn't really want her to change.

He fished out his phone and called her boss who transmitted the photo of Selim.

"We're upping the urgency, Cochran," Mercier said. "We had another message, followed by a two-hour blackout, a definite warning. This guy is good."

Chapter 6

Tess felt like a different person. She fluffed up her curls, twisted one around her finger to restore its bounce and reapplied some lipstick after brushing her teeth.

She not only looked like a stranger but felt like one, too. And this one seemed to be lacking the case of nerves that had caused her seasickness. Thank God for that! In fact, she rather liked the *Jezebel* now that she was used to being aboard.

"Got your sea legs, I see," Cameron observed when she joined him in the saloon. He had called it that, though she'd have named it a lounge. Lovely room, anyway, and outfitted at great expense. The galley at one end had stainless appliances and, in a nook on the opposite side, what looked like a state-of-the-art computer system. Cameron already had it on and had been working.

Mercier arranged for the best. As she had learned on her two former ops, he never overlooked the details. Everything she would need, including the expert.

"Learn anything new?" she asked, glancing at the screen.

Cameron nodded and leaned back in the computer chair. "There's been a blackout, which lasted two hours. He's expected to make contact soon and attempt to hurry payment. The NSA has tracked the former transmissions to an account registered to a John Eversham."

"An alias with no address," she replied, guessing.

She noted a light of excitement in his eyes. "Of course, but it's a pretty good bet he's around here, and I'll bet he's not holing up in a room between calls. Saint-Tropez's not that large, and we're lucky it's the off-season. Otherwise we'd be looking at about thirty thousand people. As it is, we can count on around a third of that. We'll go trolling. If we locate him, you can make contact."

"And if we don't find him?" she asked.

"We *have* to find him and soon. He'll think he's safe, so there's no real reason he'd take an alias except for his Internet account. Mercier's got people running checks to see if he's registered anywhere under either name. Meanwhile, we search," he replied, taking a paper from the desk and handing it to her. "Here's what he looks like, or at least what he looked like two years ago."

She took the transmitted photo and studied it. "He's just a kid. Doesn't even look twenty yet." The hacker had short, curly hair, large dark eyes and full, sensual lips. She couldn't see what he was wearing, because he was holding the identifying sign up to his chest for the picture taken when he'd been arrested. "He's almost too pretty to be a guy."

"He's twenty-six, and don't let his looks fool you. Selim's smart. He's slightly built, five-eight, works out, and he's slippery as an eel. Almost lost him a couple of times when I was tailing him in London. He sensed he was being followed, or maybe he was just paranoid. He never made me, though. I'm sure of that."

"So he wouldn't suspect anything if I just wandered over, a total stranger, and struck up a conversation?"

Cameron smiled. "You won't have to. Just make eye contact, give him that half smile of yours and look away. He'll bite."

"I don't know," she admitted. "What if he's already hooked up with someone? There must be scads of beautiful women in Saint-Tropez, certainly better looking than I'll ever be."

"Now that, I doubt. Even if he's involved, give him that look and he'll find a way."

Tess's face grew hot. "You're putting too much faith in a layer of makeup and this silly updo."

He shook his head and grinned. "It's more than that, Tess. You have a certain quality about you. Not sure what to call it, but it's like an aura of combined come-hither and hands off. A real challenge."

"For someone like *him*, you mean." She wasn't really fishing for compliments and hated that it sounded that way.

He raised his eyebrows and pursed his lips, rocking

a little in the swivel chair. After a pregnant pause, he answered. "Yeah, someone like him."

Tess forced her attention back to the photo of their mark, thinking about what Cameron had just revealed. Did she really have that quality? *Come-hither?* She couldn't help but smile. Did Cameron truly see her that way? Her gaze slid back to him.

"That's the look," he said immediately, pointing at her for emphasis. "Give him that, play him for a bit, and then reel him in."

She sighed. Well, that answered her question. Apparently it didn't work on Cameron. "So, do we wait for tonight?"

"No. We'll hit the beaches and search. It's too beautiful a day to stay inside. Maybe he'll think so, too." With that announcement, he got up and headed out on deck.

Beaches. She wasn't one for parading around nearly naked, the way she had heard they did there. The only swimming she'd ever done was at an indoor pool at the Y for lessons and in training at the academy when it was required. Her one-piece tank suit was too revealing, as far as she was concerned. And she had not purchased that bikini Mercier had suggested.

Her stomach quivered a little. She grabbed a striped silk pillow off the lounge and clutched it to her middle. Oddly enough, she didn't feel her insides lurch. She hugged the pillow tighter and took a deep breath. This wasn't so bad. Maybe if she didn't go topside, she wouldn't be sick.

It took a few more moments to realize the motion was actually soothing, not disturbing at all. Tentatively, she stood, rocking slightly from one foot to the other. Sea legs. For real, she had sea legs! If she had been just a tad more confident in them, she'd have run up to the deck and announced it to the captain! But maybe she'd just wait awhile and see if this was only a momentary respite.

Instead, she made her way to the galley end of the cabin and found ginger ale, just in case.

Cameron anchored the yacht within sight of the beach and went below to find Tess on the phone with Mercier. She rang off when he appeared and smiled up at him. "No further e-mails since you spoke with him. He's arranged a car for us, a new Mercedes. Can you believe it?"

"Good. Appearance counts as everything here. I guess he realizes that. We might not even need the car if we find him on the beaches. Can't cover them all, but we'll try the most likely ones before dark. After that, we'll start on the clubs."

"Jack said we might need reservations and offered to pull some strings if we need it. Or maybe we could use bribes."

Cameron smiled. "Not the way it works. You don't look great, you don't get in. That simple. So go put on your bikini and the filmy little wrap while I change."

She looked confused. "I don't own a bikini, and I didn't bring a cover-up. I can just throw something on over my tank suit."

"I figured as much." He headed for his cabin, tugging off his shirt as he went. "Look in the blue bag. I got some things for you when you were trying on dresses.

Wear them, and that's an order. A tank suit would get you laughed off the entire coast." He closed his door before she could argue.

"I don't care what beach we go to, I'm not going topless!" she called out, making him laugh out loud.

He quickly changed into the brief little suit he had kept since the op he'd had in Australia a few years ago. Talk about getting laughed outta town! He could only imagine the hoots he'd get wearing it on the Tybee beach. The damn thing barely covered his essentials. He sympathized with Tess having to don a tiny bikini. But he couldn't wait to see her in it all the same.

He was waiting in the saloon when she came out. The cover-up was nearly transparent and revealed her knockout figure. He'd known she had a body, of course, but he couldn't take his eyes off her. "Wow. That ought to get us a ticket anywhere we want to go. You look smashing."

She blushed beneath the tan and ducked her head. A curl tumbled over one eye. "I feel ridiculous."

Her suit was bronze, nearly the color of her skin. She wore the large gold earrings he'd bought her, as well as the shiny little sandals that matched her suit. The thigh-length shirt was golden gauze with a subtle satin stripe.

"You look…rich. Try to feel that way. Move like a star and they'll think you are one. Head back, chin and chest out. Think bored indolence, too sexy for your clothes."

She was too busy looking at him. He had left his white, collarless shirt open over his suit. "What's the matter?" he asked, wondering if he'd forgotten something.

"Uh…towels." Blushing again. The red glowed right through her tan. He loved it.

He grinned. "Surely you don't think we're going to get *wet*. And take off your watch."

"Why? You're wearing yours."

"Because it's a statement," he explained. "Our cachet. The Rolex is as necessary as having money. Maybe more. I should have picked you up a knockoff in Nice."

She wrestled off the Timex impatiently and laid it on the table. "There."

"Good girl. Now we're in business. Remember your persona. Rich bitch out to show off."

"And you?" she demanded.

"Boy toy slash bodyguard. Don't you love it?" He struck a pose, laughed and ushered her up on deck. "Let go and enjoy this, Tess. It's part of the package. If you don't love what you do, you might as well quit and let somebody else do it, right?"

She huffed. "I think you're entirely too into all this."

"Done it before, that's all. Liked it then, too." It sure beat tailing somebody through the dark side of London or Paris. And it was a damn sight better than trolling for fish off Tybee with a couple of fat guys on vacation.

"When are we landing the boat?" she asked as she looked out over the three-mile stretch of beach.

"Docking? We'll do that later tonight." He headed for the bridge to blow the boat's horn. "A water taxi will be out to pick us up. This is faster than docking and then driving out from town."

"And it's just the *done thing,* right?" she asked with a little laugh.

"Showmanship's the name of the game."

When the little powerboat arrived, Cameron noted

that Tess had worked herself up to the role. She played it a little too haughty but, all in all, gave the impression he had asked her to.

He directed the water-taxi operator to the southern end of Pampelonne, motioning him to avoid L'Aqua Club, a gay hangout, and bring them in at Le Club 55. They disembarked, tipped the water-taxi operator and made their way to the club's restaurant. "We'll check here first. You hungry?"

"Coffee would be good." She tossed her hair and scanned the rows of people lunching and sunning themselves on mats. He knew she was looking for any guy the right size and complexion to be their man.

The Moorish-style restaurant surrounded a pleasant courtyard. It was relatively small and business was slow. They hurried through their cappuccino, checked out the customers and left, strolling along hand in hand, scanning faces for an Egyptian playboy.

It was a long walk, but the sand was beautifully groomed, and the human scenery something to behold. Eventually they ran out of well-swept beach and had to watch their step.

"Warning," he said in a low voice as they neared the middle section of Pampelonne Beach. "Nudity abounds. Keep your cool."

"I'm not a child, Cochran!" she exclaimed, stopping to whisk off the gauzy shirt and drape it over one arm. "I've already seen enough skin today to immunize me against shock."

"I doubt we'll find him here. Mostly Northern Europeans out to strut their stuff. Look anyway."

"Thank God for sunglasses," she muttered, adjusting them as she spoke. "How long is this beach, anyway?"

"About three miles total, but we don't have to walk back. We'll taxi back to the *Jezebel* after we've covered Tahiti Beach."

"This is hopeless," she said with a sigh. "We've checked out nearly a dozen restaurants, and my eyes are crossing. All the faces are looking the same. All the bodies, too, for that matter."

"I know what you mean, but we'll soon be through Moorea and onto Tahiti Beach. I think the bodies are getting better," he said, laughing and giving her an affectionate one-armed hug. He let his hand slide to her waist.

She stiffened a little, but then relaxed as he brought his hand up to the back of her neck and massaged it gently. He admired her effort to adapt. She was becoming a little more at ease with him, he thought, or maybe she was covering her uneasiness better than before. At any rate, she was trying really hard, and he appreciated it.

He couldn't quite figure whether she was unused to being touched by a man or if it was just *his* touch that made her nervous. The former, he hoped.

Tahiti Beach was busier than the others, but not exactly teeming this time of year. The weather was perfect, but fewer people took vacations in the fall, preferring the heat of the summer sun.

"There!" she exclaimed, catching his arm and nodding toward a group of four arguing in French. "Is that him?"

Cameron guided her over for a closer look, noted the features of the only guy who could be Selim. "Close but no cigar."

The search ate up hours as the sun sank low.

"We'll never find him this way. And I'm exhausted," she said. "My calves are screaming from walking in the sand. Aren't yours?"

"It has been a long day," he agreed. "Let's head back to the boat, grab a bite to eat and rest a little before we go out tonight." He glanced at his watch and decided they could take a few hours to regroup. Nothing really cranked up until after ten, anyway.

"I've read that reservations are required almost everywhere. Maybe Jack will know by now if he's on any of the clubs' lists."

"Unfortunately, you really don't have to be to get in if the door guys in charge like your looks. And Selim *is* pretty. You said so yourself."

"You just know everything, don't you? Why am I even here?"

"Eye candy, of course." He laughed when she punched him in the side. "Hey! It's a compliment."

She snorted. "After all the naked women you've ogled today, you're complimenting the number one prude?"

He took her shirt from her and held it out so she could put it on. "A little left to the imagination's not a bad thing. You notice I didn't bare it all, either."

Her smile was slow, almost reticent, as mysterious and seductive as the Mona Lisa's, that very one he had encouraged earlier.

Better be careful and not delve into that mystery, he warned himself as they hopped on the taxi and sped out to the yacht.

Where they would be entirely alone for a couple of

hours. Maybe he should have thought of that a little bit sooner.

Cameron didn't want to take advantage of their situation. Nor did he want to make Tess uncomfortable. To that end, he firmly decided to keep his distance, keep his hands off of her and his mind on the business at hand.

But what if she wanted him to take advantage? That devil on his shoulder could be a real pain in the ass, but it stirred up doubts all the same. What if she was too shy to make a move?

Tess studied the photograph of Selim again after she had dressed for the evening. She needed the distraction as she waited for Cameron to pay for their berth in the marina, send for their car and return to the yacht. It took every ounce of her will not to think about him instead of the mission.

Those perfect abs, thighs like tree trunks, the way that Speedo had fit. She shook her head to clear the total image of Cameron the Boy Toy.

She smoothed the skirt of the silky halter dress and missed feeling a panty line. Thongs were the pits, only marginally better than going totally bare. The push-up bra felt like a vise, but her *girls* were on display like they'd never been before. She took a fortifying breath and ignored their vicarious rise along the plunging neckline.

Her naked back tingled. *Probably with anticipation,* she figured. How would his palm feel against her skin tonight? There had been several tentative brushes of it when she'd had her shirt off on the beach. Man, she had to get over this in a hurry.

"Hey, Tess, you ready?" he called from the saloon.

"Out in a minute," she called back. She tottered into the bathroom on her four-inch heels and checked her lipstick one last time, tugged an errant curl back into place and adjusted the draped fabric barely covering the lower half of her breasts. Okay. She'd do.

She hurried to the door of her cabin, then stopped, took another deep breath, forced herself to go slowly and become what he expected.

The look on his face was worth it. Tess raised her chin, expanded her chest and looked down her nose at him. "Close your mouth. You look like a guppy," she said in her haughtiest tone.

He laughed uproariously. Not the response she was after. When he got over it, he shook his head. "You'll need a bodyguard, for real!"

"Thanks," she said with a genuine smile. "What do you think, really?"

"You might not even need the special smile," he replied with a wry grin. "Let's go find Selim and see what he thinks. Got your cell phone?"

She nodded, held up the small clutch purse, and they were off. Tess resisted any comment on Cameron's attire. It was perfectly unobtrusive in and of itself. His suit was gray, the shirt a silvery, lighter shade, and he wore no tie.

He had slicked back his hair and confined it in a short ponytail. That style exposed his rather square face and emphasized the strong features. He looked the part of a bodyguard and had already assumed the attitude.

No, the clothes weren't what one noted first. The first impression was that he exuded danger like a loaded pistol. Her bodyguard.

"Are you armed?" she asked as they walked down the quayside to the waiting Mercedes.

"To the teeth," he admitted. "I won't ask if you are, since there's no place on that getup to hide a weapon."

She shot him the half smile and lowered her voice an octave. "Darling, I *am* the weapon."

Yeah, that got her a speechless double take. She was in character. How empowering! The way he looked at her was so totally different from before, as if he had brand-new regard for her, a surprised regard. Tess almost laughed out loud.

Her body felt different than it ever had, her movements more liquid, and every cell was alive and tingling with anticipation for what came next. *Sexy,* she realized. This was the very first time she had ever allowed herself to feel sexy. Now that she had a perfectly good reason, it was okay. Necessary.

Maybe she wouldn't go back to her old self at all now that she'd shed that self-imposed reserve. She didn't have to be promiscuous, of course, but it felt damn good to have a man see her as desirable. Pretty. She felt pretty and powerful in a way she never had before.

Cameron had been right. Altering her appearance had changed her.

She felt as if her very cells had changed, that her body had a sensuousness she had never paid attention to or hadn't even known was there.

Her breasts felt fuller. And they certainly looked it.

The silk of the most expensive dress she had ever worn caressed her skin every time she moved. Actually encouraged her to move more than usual.

This was crazy. Amazing, but crazy. And she had to get a hold on this nonsense.

There was a certain intoxication to these new feelings, which she had to be aware of and avoid. She was on a mission, in disguise, and had a job to perform. Later, she would dissect this persona and decide whether any of it was worth keeping.

Once on their way in the Mercedes, Tess allowed herself to feel rich, beautiful and privileged. It was the role she had to assume, and she would play it for all it was worth.

The ride was luxurious on soft, supple leather, with muted music drifting from who knew how many hidden speakers and that wonderful new car smell, which made her want a luxury vehicle. She refused to think about her six-year-old Mazda.

"I could *so* become a material girl," she muttered, making him laugh again.

"Okay, where to first?" she asked as he maneuvered the car along the winding streets of the ancient fishing village turned glitzy tourist mecca.

"La Bodega de Papagayo, if it's still open this late in the year," he replied. "Caters to the twenty something crowd. Might not be sophisticated enough for our boy, but it's worth a shot."

It was operating, full steam ahead, with people waiting to get in, some looking disgruntled as they were turned away.

"Smile at the bouncer," Cameron advised. "If he doesn't like us, we don't get in."

Tess made a show of getting out of the Mercedes as Cameron held the door for her. She bent over, displaying her pushed-up cleavage, as well as showing a bit of leg, hoping that would help. Then she realized that such displays in a town where nudity was commonplace were pretty tame and no real treat for the locals. Maybe the expensive car would make a good impression.

She smiled sweetly at the doorman, who grinned back, showing her his gold tooth and practiced leer. When he motioned them past the line waiting for approval, Cameron slipped him a bill and they were in. That seemed more like a token of thanks than a bribe, since it had been given after the fact.

La Bodega wasn't a large place, only two rooms, but it was packed with people and the dancing was wild. The music and the excitement were insidious. Tess found herself wishing there was no mission, no search, that she was simply there to enjoy.

She and Cameron stayed together as they searched.

Tess had gotten used to Cameron handling her, with a hand on her waist, a one-armed embrace, even that palm on her back, which she had anticipated earlier. His touch had begun to feel natural now. *And exciting,* she admitted.

She should keep firmly in mind why they were here and what she had to do. *But why not enjoy it a little, too?*

Something inside her really had shifted, and she had unleashed a part of herself she had spent most of her life denying or suppressing. She kept telling herself it was only that this pretense had given her permission to accept that aspect.

It should be temporary, only for the duration of this operation. When it was over, she would go back to the way she was before and forget this high-maintenance look and attitude. This freedom to feel a bit wild.

But was that because she thought she *should* change back or because she wanted to? Did she really want to?

Maybe she couldn't convince herself, simply because she liked doing this and being this way.

And what about Cameron? Could he be the reason she liked it? The old Tess was careful, reserved and a self-confessed loner.

She looked at the breath-stealing man beside her and felt the definite punch of desire. The new Tess wasn't any of those things.

Chapter 7

Tess forced herself to concentrate on the search. Patrons of La Bodega were so diverse, yet so much alike, way past tipsy, living the good life to the hilt. Most of them weren't chronologically younger than she was, and yet they seemed so.

Cameron should have appeared out of place, but somehow he didn't. If she were seeing him for the first time, he would stand out in this crowd, but only because his looks were striking even in a sea of beautiful people. He seemed to fit everywhere without really blending in.

"Well, he's not here," Cameron said once they had made the rounds twice. "Let's go."

They returned to the front, retrieved the car and were off again. They hit two more clubs, were admitted without any problems and found no one resembling the man they were after. "Where to next?" she asked, tamping down her excitement so she wouldn't appear awed by it all. Cameron seemed so unaffected, as if he'd been born to this lifestyle. No wonder experience counted so much in this business. Well, she was gaining it, wasn't she?

Professional experience was one thing, personal experience another. She hadn't much in that last category, either, and didn't quite know what to think of the mixed signals she was getting from Cameron.

She would glance across the crowd and catch him watching her with a look of such intense heat she thought she might melt on the spot, yet when they came together to compare notes, he acted the cool professional agent.

He would touch her hand, her arm, her bare back and it seemed more like caresses than not. Her skin tingled. Her heart thundered with the pounding beat of the music, an urgent sexual rhythm. She ached to touch him back, to feel those hands all over her. But then the cursory glances that went with his touches were unreadable as he continued searching for Selim.

This had been going on all night and tension had mounted so powerfully by this time that Tess felt wired for anything. Hot-wired. Absolutely ready. Did he know what he was doing to her? How distracting it was?

She did her best to shake off the feelings of arousal and concentrate on what she had to accomplish here. He's doing the same, a wicked little voice chimed in her brain. She didn't trust it for a hot second.

And then he looked down at her, not a mere glance this time, and he smiled.

"That was the last stop," he said. "We can't possibly make them all in one evening, anyway. I don't know about you, but I'm ready to call it a night."

"And you're not even wearing high heels." Tess slipped her arm through his, and they went out to wait for the valet to bring the car around.

He placed his hand over hers and gave it a meaningful squeeze. "You're doing great," he whispered.

The trip back to the marina was short. When they got there, he parked and turned to her. "Think you can do all this again tomorrow?"

"Do we have a choice?" she asked with a sigh, leaning back against the headrest.

He had turned, his elbow propped on the steering wheel. "C'mon, admit it. You love it here. Imagine how lovely it would be if we weren't working."

"But we are," she said, rolling her head to face him. "It would have been nice to have a glass of wine, dance a little. The music was fantastic, wasn't it?"

"Yeah. So are you, Tess." He leaned over and kissed her gently on the lips. "Absolutely fantastic," he whispered.

She kissed him back, not so gently, inhaling his scent, reveling in the taste of him and the feel of his mouth on hers. The heady rush of lust made her dizzy. When he finally drew away, they were both breathing heavily. He brushed her cheek with his hand and smiled.

Wordlessly, they got out of the car, walked hand in hand to the dock, and he helped her onto the boat. She knew what he expected to happen next. She knew what she *wanted* to happen next. Would he turn it off again and go all businesslike on her?

As soon as they reached the saloon, he took her in his arms and kissed her again. "I want you," he whispered.

Not *I love you*. She would not have been fooled by those words, but these echoed her need precisely; she found she didn't care about waiting for love. How would she know if a man loved her, anyway, when they almost always lied to get sex? At least he was honest. He wanted her.

"I want you, too," she said and meant every word of it. She was about to take a little walk on the wild side for a change. Surely she had it coming to her after being straitlaced for so long. Cameron made her feel safe. He wouldn't hurt her. He wouldn't lie.

She was well aware that the woman he really wanted was the prettied-up version he had created with fancy hair, a fake tan and the push-up bra, which was cutting into her flesh like dull knives.

"Let's undress," she said. "I'm miserable."

She felt more than heard his laughter. "You always surprise the hell out of me," he said. He scooped her up as if she weighed nothing and took her to the master cabin, following her down to the berth so that he lay half on top of her.

When he moved in to kiss her, she pushed at his chest. "I have to wear this again tomorrow night, so don't rip it off, okay?"

He sat up and gave her the sweetest smile. "I have *never* in my life ripped clothes off a woman. How gauche would that be? Undressing is foreplay. Why miss out on that?"

Then he said something in Italian that sounded really enticing. Tess wished she knew the language. All she understood was *carissima*. An endearment. So the big, bad Cochran was a romantic at heart, or at least on the surface. Either way, for her benefit. How sweet was that?

She watched with fascination as he reached down and removed her shoes, taking time to caress one half-numb foot, then the other. That felt so heavenly, she groaned.

His hand traveled up her leg, beneath the silken skirt of her dress and rested for a moment on her hip. One teasing finger slipped beneath the strap at the side of her thong. His lazy gaze never left hers.

Tess saw right into his mind in that instant, as if he had opened up to her on purpose, an offering of trust, a gift. She saw raw anticipation. She saw all that he imagined they would do together. She saw need that stretched beyond the night. Tantalizing. And erotic.

Slowly, he removed his hand from beneath the dress, caressing her leg as he began to lift the hem. She sat up a little. He slid his arms around her and unzipped, still in no great hurry. The silk brushed her nerve endings, making her skin tingle wherever it touched. When he drew the dress over her head and carefully laid it aside, Tess shivered with eagerness.

"Cold?" he asked, trailing one finger over her shoulder and down between her breasts.

She shook her head, still holding his gaze. "Now you."

He removed his shoes, then stood and slipped off his jacket, letting it fall to the floor beside him.

Then he removed the gun from the back of his belt, twirled it once on his finger, caught it fast in his grip and grinned. Tess laughed at the antic as he carefully laid his weapon aside. He was making this fun, and she was thoroughly into it. She clapped her hands slowly and waited for more.

Strong fingers worked the buttons of his shirt, and he took that off as well. She had seen him without it before, but not like this. Not in a bedroom, with her half naked and his eyes on her reaction. She pursed her lips in a silent whistle.

Tess sighed audibly at the sight of that massive chest, with its tightly drawn nipples and dusting of dark brown curls. He unbuckled his belt and slid it slowly out of the loops, dropping it to one side as he worked the fastener and unzipped his pants. There was a pause as he raised one eyebrow in question. Tess nodded. Then he dropped the pants and stepped out of them.

His dark blue briefs hardly concealed anything; in fact, they emphasized everything. Was this how women got off on male strippers? She had never seen one in action for real, but it couldn't be any more provocative than this.

Obviously at ease with his state of undress, he joined her on the berth, sitting beside her as she lay propped on the pillows. He looked pointedly at her bra. "That has served its purpose for tonight, don't you think?"

He snaked one hand beneath her back and unsnapped the fastener with expertise. Tess did not want to consider how many times he had practiced that particular move. He brushed the straps off her shoulders and pulled the cups away from her breasts.

For a long moment, he just looked at her. "You're excited," he said, raising that eyebrow again.

"So are you," she said, looking down at the blatant evidence of that.

"You're not going to say no," he said. It wasn't a question.

"I would have said it long before now," she admitted. To reinforce her willingness, she removed the thong and dropped it over the side of the berth.

"No regrets in the morning?" he asked, as if that would be a condition. He stripped off his briefs.

Oh my. She tried not to stare.

"No regrets ever," she promised. This was what it was. Sex for the sake of sex. Odd that she didn't feel promiscuous. She should, but instead she felt…free. Free of the old rules she had made for herself, since no one else had bothered to make any for her. Free of the self-doubt that had held her prisoner for so long. Cameron might not love her, but he had freed her. No, there would be no regrets. None at all.

She held out her arms, and he came over her, bracing on his elbows as he lowered his body onto hers, a delicious weight, unfamiliar yet comfortable. Comforting.

"I didn't plan for this," she murmured as he nuzzled her breasts. "You have protection?"

He abandoned his quest for the moment and looked up at her. "I do."

"So you gave this some thought before?"

"Since I first saw you on the dock at Tybee," he said.

Maybe so, but she suspected he had gotten condoms in the men's room at one of the clubs. "Pretty sure of yourself, aren't you?"

"Hope springs eternal," he confessed with a smile. "Aren't you glad?"

"Elated. Ah, do that again."

He moved against her as he returned his attention to her breasts, caressing her lower body with his as he stoked the fire between them.

Tess let herself go, loving the small surprises he plied with his mouth and tongue, even as she wished he would hurry.

But Cameron was obviously not a fan of speed. A man with a slow hand. The words to an old tune from years ago ran through her mind. She loved slow.

The night was perfect, with the lazy splash of waves, the cozy comfort of the lavish cabin that cocooned them, the lovely scent of his skin and the feel of it as she kissed him. Sheer perfection. If he only would get on with it.

But he took her higher, made her want more, stirred in her a need she had never known before.

At last, he drew back, kneeling above her to don the protection. Instead of an interruption of pleasure, that, too, became a part of the teasing prologue. Emboldened by his openness, she reached out and smoothed down the roll of latex until he was covered. He remained where he was, looking down at her as she stroked him.

Unhurried as ever, he took her hand and laced his fingers through hers as he lowered himself again and entered her. She lifted her hips to make him thrust, but he controlled the foray until fully seated inside her.

She almost cried out with frustration, contracting around him with a fury. He slowly withdrew all the way, then sank into her again with maddening control.

He stroked once, twice and then again. Tess cried out, the pleasure too keen.

Her mind still soaring, she felt him begin thrusting faster and harder, his control slipping by degrees, pushing her faster and faster to the edge of reason. Suddenly she reached a pinnacle, and they plunged together, a free fall that stole her breath and shook her so violently, she wept.

Finally, he withdrew and held her close, whispering something that sounded tender and comforting, though she missed the words. She hadn't the strength to imagine it was anything to do with love. But it was enough. She closed her eyes, stroked his wide shoulders and drifted into sleep, glad she was in his arms. No, no regrets at all.

Morning crept in through the window, throwing weak sunlight across the bed. Tess knew she was alone before she opened her eyes and was glad of that, she told herself.

Who wanted to face a new lover with mascara smudged beneath her eyes and her hair a messy tangle? She rolled out of bed and went to repair the damage. After a shower and quick shampoo, she wrapped a towel around her body, another around her hair, brushed her teeth and went back in the cabin to find something to wear.

She decided not to think about last night. They had both known that it would happen, and it had. No need to rehash it. In the light of day, that might make them both uncomfortable.

But, oh, when she thought of that body of his, the smooth silk over steel muscles, the way he moved, his hands. Those wonderful hands. She groaned low in her throat just remembering....

He opened the door a crack and, without looking in, said, "Put on your suit. We're checking out the smaller beaches this morning."

So much for reflection on his part. He'd probably forgotten the details before his feet hit the floor.

"Good morning to you, too," she muttered as she snatched up the bikini she had left lying across the chair yesterday.

All business again, was he? She desperately needed to keep a strong check on her emotions so she could act that way, too. Maybe he gave lessons. She yanked on the suit, cursing when the strap twisted.

"Not a morning person, huh," he said on the other side of the door. "I bring coffee." His hand, holding a mug, appeared through the partially open door.

"Oh, for Pete's sake, come in."

He was smiling and looking like a cool million when he entered. And he was wearing only his swimsuit. Tess closed her eyes against the sight, but it wasn't working.

"Take the coffee and let me help you out there," he suggested.

Tess took the mug and turned around, sipping the strong black brew as he straightened her strap and brushed his palm over her back. "You have dimples just above your cheeks." He touched one with his finger. "Devilishly cute."

"Beat it while I fix my hair. I'll be out in ten," she said, a little miffed that he could look so good, while she needed time to look halfway decent.

He started out. "Want an omelet or fruit?" he asked as he went.

"Toast. And more coffee. Does anything rattle you, Cochran?" she demanded.

He laughed. "You do. Like a maraca, babe. The trick was to wake up before you did this morning and work out for a while. By the way, the raccoon look was sweet on you. I watched you sleep."

She almost threw the mug at him. *Infuriating man!* But she couldn't quite contain the smile. She'd had only one other morning after. This one was going infinitely better, even with the teasing. Probably because of it.

She had rattled Cameron. *Like a maraca. How 'bout that?*

This trip to the beaches proved no more eventful than the one they'd made the day before. The search was a bit easier in that there weren't as many faces to scan, but Cameron found that keeping his eyes off Tess was the hardest part.

Wasn't it odd how much more at ease she seemed with him and with herself? He had expected awkwardness between them today, after making love with her last night. He had worried about it. She obviously wasn't used to falling into bed with someone on impulse. In fact, he'd bet she hadn't had more than one or two lovers before this.

Her inexperience was a definite turn-on, but that wasn't what had prompted him to make a play. She had really wanted him, too, and he knew it. Not just sex, but *him* in particular. Yet she didn't seem to have any expectations, either of another bout in the bedroom or a future relationship. He couldn't quite figure her out. What exactly *did* she want?

Whatever it was, he wanted her to have it. That, too, seemed odd. Why such a blinding need to please this woman at all cost? Didn't make sense, given his past involvement. Brenda was in total eclipse.

And why was it that everything Tess did, however innocent, seemed sexy or endearing, or both? Man, you'd think he was falling for her or something.

She was just standing there now, her gaze traveling from stranger to stranger as she idly licked at the cone of Italian ice cream he'd bought her. It was damned difficult to keep from getting hot just watching her.

"There," she said, tossing the ice cream and pointing down the beach. "Could be him."

They took off, walking faster than usual to catch up. The guy they were following veered off the beach and disappeared in the surrounding vegetation. They followed the path through the trees and emerged on the far side of the tree line in time to see him hop into a speedboat docked there in an inlet. He was gone before they could see his face.

"What do you think?" Tess asked.

"Right size, moved like him. Could have been." Cameron checked the time. "Let's go back to the marina. I think we've covered about as much ground as we can. We'll stop for dinner, catch a nap and go back out tonight."

She stopped and looked up at him. "About the nap part…Cameron, I think we'd better not, well, you know. No regrets, I swear, but this could get in the way if we let it."

"Yeah, I know. You're probably right." He continued

back to the beach, mostly so he wouldn't have to look at her when they had this discussion. She was right and he knew it.

He'd had sex with women he worked with before, but Tess was different. She had gotten into his mind and was playing with his concentration.

He had to compartmentalize big-time for the duration of the mission. Put off whatever this little affair might turn into eventually. It was too intense to pursue it right now. However, he couldn't let it go. "Could I maybe give you a call or something after we get back to the world?"

She nodded. "Back to the world. Odd how that describes it so well."

He hadn't thought much about it. It was a common phrase used by agents, even soldiers coming off assignment, especially when they were out of country. Last night had been out of this world, that was for sure. He felt like an alien inside himself, one with all sorts of feelings he hadn't experienced before.

He tried not to compare Tess to Brenda, the woman he had once thought he loved. Still, the two things they had in common were impossible to ignore. They were both career-oriented government agents, and they were both smart and efficient.

They were both beautiful, too, but not in the same ways. Tess's beauty came from inside, radiating out. Brenda's had been all surface and no substance, though it had taken him a while to see that. She had been hot, all right, but with no real warmth. Why hadn't he realized that at the time? The fact that he hadn't, ought to make him doubt his assessment of Tess, but it didn't.

He *knew* her in ways he had never known Brenda. The thing was, Tess *let* him know her. She was so special, he could never know enough about her to satisfy himself. He wanted years to learn more.

She was looking at him strangely as they walked side by side in the sand. "Are you okay with it, Cam?"

When had anyone called him Cam? Not since he was a kid. "Sure," he said. "So will it be all right if I call you?"

She shrugged. "Who knows what will happen between now and then? Last night was what it was. Let's leave it at that for now."

Cameron tried to tamp down his disappointment. And he had worried about *her* reaction to their sleeping together? He should have paid more attention to how involved he was getting.

The remainder of the afternoon passed swiftly and without incident. Tess called a report in to Control. Nothing new from there.

She tried not to think about how Cameron felt or the fact that she'd been able to read him last night, even a little this morning. She had picked up on his confusion concerning the two of them, maybe some anger there, too, but she wasn't sure whether it was directed at himself or her.

Every now and then she would catch a flash of what he was thinking. But then, she wasn't always certain whether what she sensed was a feeling he was having or one she was projecting.

She managed to redo her hair with the curling iron she'd brought with her. Her dress had survived intact, and the shoes still hurt her feet.

"Did I overdo the makeup?" she asked Cameron when she emerged from her cabin.

"Looks perfect." He reached up and rearranged a curl with a little tug. Then he lifted her chin with one finger and brushed his thumb just below her bottom lip. She leaned into his touch, unable to help herself.

He had closed her out now. She couldn't tell whether the gesture was one of intimacy and affection or if he was merely sprucing up her disguise. She hoped…

"Okay, sport, let's go find him," he said, breaking the spell.

Chapter 8

At another marina far away, a man accessed his wireless connection. He laughed when he saw the codes had changed again. He wondered if another little blackout would get things moving faster on the financial front. Fingertips resting on the keys, he paused to think it through. At least it would show them that they couldn't outfox him.

But no, he would wait. The latest report through channels declared that the matter was being settled, so no further blackouts were needed right now. Funds were being amassed. He would check the Swiss account tomorrow and see if there had been a deposit.

Getting the money out might pose a few problems, but he was in no hurry. Once he cut the power, they would be in such a stew that monitoring the Swiss account would drop pretty low on their list of priorities.

Instead of dousing their lights again, he'd just give them a little shove with another warning message tonight.

What a stroke of genius. The boy he'd chosen to take the heat was Egyptian, persona non grata in his own family, virtually broke and the perfect example of a greedy little terrorist.

He finished the message and logged off. Might as well get dressed, go out on the town and enjoy the evening since he would soon be moving on.

Fort-de-France had looked so perfect when he'd sailed in a few months ago, but like everywhere else he had docked in the last couple of years, the up-close and personal view disappointed.

He smiled and stretched, looking across the water at the old city. At least it had electricity!

"Where to first?" Tess asked when Cameron was behind the wheel and backing out of the parking space.

"Hôtel Byblos."

He drove, obviously lost in thoughts she couldn't determine, until he turned onto Avenue Paul-Signac. "Les Caves du Roy. It's bigger, the busiest disco and the most difficult to cover. Fortunately, it's Tuesday and off-season."

He pulled up to the hotel and waited for the valet. "It'll be deafening. Jack-E's a wild DJ, so put your cell on vibrate and carry it in your hand. Am I on your speed dial?"

"Not yet. I'll fix that." She pulled out her cell phone. "Okay, you're number one," she assured him when she'd programmed her phone.

"This time we'll separate after we go in. Buzz me if you hit pay dirt. I'll do the same. Work your way to the back. Then you go right and I'll go left. Try to cover the crowd to the middle as you go. It's okay to appear that you're looking for someone. Most everybody will be if they're not already hooked up."

"But don't get distracted by celebrities," she added with a grin, repeating a suggestion he had made before last night's search. "Can I squeal once if I see Johnny Depp?"

He didn't smile. "Only if you want my gun to his head."

She noted his sense of humor was on leave at the moment. "No squealing then."

"Good," he said as the valet opened her door.

She got out and headed for the entrance, not waiting for him to accompany her.

He caught up just as she reached the door. "The cover charge," he whispered right behind her ear.

Tess hadn't thought of that. The doorman looked them over and gave them the nod. She noted the denominations as Cameron whipped out several bills and handed them over. *Two hundred and fifty euros? My God.*

"Stop frowning," he warned, ushered her inside, then promptly disappeared.

Tess pasted on a bored smile and snaked her way through the crowd to the far end of the club, checking out faces as she went. The music was loud enough to wake the dead. She heartily wished for earplugs, but they probably wouldn't help. The reverberations went right through to the bone.

Enormous fountains of light flowered nearly to the ceiling. The thunder of music, crowd noise and rowdy laughter vibrated through her body, while the mixed scents of perfume, liquor and body odor assaulted her nose.

She scanned one male after another, pausing only whenever a slight, dark-haired one would fit the profile of Selim.

Tess moved more slowly on her return through the club. Several men spoke to her as she passed, but she ignored them.

Selim's face in the photograph totally occupied her mind as she searched. "Where the devil are you?" she muttered under her breath.

And suddenly as that, there he was, as if she'd conjured him up out of thin air. Big as life, he was standing almost directly in front of her. And he, too, was searching for someone.

Tess quickly buzzed Cameron on the phone with her thumb and hurried to brush past Selim. *"Excusez-moi, s'il vous plaît,"* she said, meeting his gaze. Their eyes met and held. She remember to use the half smile and add the unspoken invitation.

"Certainment," he replied suggestively, moving closer. Then, suddenly recalling something, he gave a helpless shrug and reluctantly turned away from her.

She kept him in sight as he made his way through the throng to the upper level, where the tables were.

Tess had *known* why he left the moment he did it, she realized, amazed at herself. Seldom before had she been able to read anyone without their knowledge and cooperation. She didn't count last night with Cameron. She had the distinct feeling he had *let* her.

Yet she had picked up on Zahi Selim's thoughts, as

if he'd spoken them out loud. But it wasn't words in his mind that she had gotten. It was only his intent she'd grasped, most likely because he thought in his mother tongue and not in English.

He had definitely been interested in her, fully intending to speak to her, to start up something, then highly frustrated that he had something more crucial to do. Someone he must meet right then.

"You rang?" Cameron said as he reached her side.

"It's…it's *him!*" she said, without taking her eyes off their subject's back. "I can't believe we did it, Cam. We actually found him! It's Selim."

"No kidding."

"He's going up there to meet somebody." Tess pointed.

"You're sure it's him?" Cameron demanded.

"Absolutely. We actually spoke. Then he rushed off. I had him interested, but then he had to go."

"A date maybe," Cameron said, his mouth close to her ear. "Or maybe not. Let's see who it is. Move on up there so you can get a closer look. Go slowly. In character, Tess."

She obeyed, hard to do since she was so eager to get where she was going. Her eyes never left the mark.

Selim took a seat at a table with another man, a heavyset fellow with white hair who looked remarkably like the disc jockey she'd seen operating the turntable. But it wasn't him. The music kept flowing, changing as the raucous voice of Jack-E bellowed something unintelligible over the microphone.

Tess bypassed the table and turned when she had Selim's back to her. The other man was tapping on the table, as if to make a point of something he was saying.

Selim nodded, pushed away and stood up again. The other man sat back, as if satisfied. This one she couldn't read. He cast her a passing glance, then looked away.

Tess opened her phone, photographed the dancers below them and spanned left, quickly capturing the face of Selim's friend. Now he was busy watching Selim head back to the front of the club.

She raised her arm and waved in the direction of the entrance, as if recognizing someone she knew, hoping to alert Cameron. Then she hurried after Selim.

He was a good twenty feet in front of her, and she saw Cameron well ahead of him. They wouldn't lose him now! But she still had to meet him somehow and persuade him to join her on the yacht.

Cameron was waiting just outside the exit. "Selim's hailing a cab, and we have to wait for the car. Damn it, where is that valet?"

"I'm on it," Tess declared and rushed toward Selim.

"Tess, wait!" she heard him say but ignored it. Their subject was about to disappear.

"Taxi!" she called, raising her arm and waving.

Selim turned, his hand on the door of the cab. "Mademoiselle?"

She turned on the charm. "Ah. Well, then, this one is yours, isn't it! Now I must wait for another."

"Nonsense. You will share with me. You are American, non?"

"No, actually, I'm Canadian. Are you certain you don't mind sharing?"

"Of course not. It will be my pleasure. Where do you go?"

"The marina. My yacht is docked there," she told him. "The person I was supposed to meet at Les Caves never showed."

Selim smiled sweetly. "Then he must have died along the way. I cannot imagine another reason to desert so beautiful a woman."

"My, you are a bit of old-world charm, aren't you?" She held out her hand, trying to delay their departure long enough for Cameron to get the car so he could follow. "I am Tessa. And you are…?"

He raised her hand to his lips as he held her gaze. "Zahi. My friends call me Zee."

How faux cosmopolitan, she thought. "Zee it is, then."

The cabdriver cleared his throat noisily, and Selim laughed, displaying dimples and blindingly white teeth. He was cute; she had to give him that. His features were attractive, but his moves seemed both copied and practiced. Watched too many James Bond movies, she'd bet. The panache was a trifle overdone.

She sensed insecurity and great determination to hide it. He had probably been a baby-faced, geeky kid who depended on his family wealth to insure whatever popularity he had enjoyed with girls. Now he wanted to make up for lost time.

"Come, my dear. We must go," he said, ushering her into the cab with a flourish of his hand.

Tess glanced through the window to see Cameron frowning thunderously at her. He was still waiting for the attendant to bring the car. He held up his phone and gave her a pointed, teeth-gritting look.

She nodded once to signal that she understood. She

punched the number on her phone to ring him and left
the line open so he could listen in on her conversation
with Selim.

"Who was that man?" Selim asked after he'd given
directions to the driver in French. "Is he the one you
were to meet?"

"Oh, no. He's simply a guard my father hired to look
after me. I signaled him to take the night off and indicated I will call if I need him."

"He takes his job lightly then, but no matter. I will
see that you are safe," Selim declared. "Now, what is the
name of this doting father who believes you need
personal protection?"

Tess took a deep breath and tried to look mysterious.
"I'd rather not say."

"He owns this yacht you go to?" Selim asked,
pressing for information, taking her hand in his.

She detected no suspicion, just sexual interest. And
greed. "No," she said with a studied blink. "*I* own the
yacht. It was a present for my birthday. My father and
his yacht are cruising the Greek islands."

Tess could almost see the dollar signs in his dark
brown eyes. Or euro signs, anyway.

She decided not to issue an invitation to accompany
her to the boat just yet. He wouldn't expect such trust
after having just met.

"So, Zee, do you live here in Saint-Tropez?" she
asked. Maybe he'd tell her where exactly. Cameron
would love an address so he could pick up the computer.

"I do," he admitted. "At least for the moment. A

friend of mine is traveling, and I am house-sitting for him. My home is in London."

"A dreadfully dull place," Tess said, glancing out the window at the passing scenery.

She hoped to God Cameron was following, because she had not been able to keep track of street signs without seeming obvious about it.

It wasn't that she didn't think she could take care of herself. She had been doing so for years and had enough training in physical defense to prevail in almost any situation. She had to admit, however, that she had never been in a position to put her skills to a real test against someone with a serious intent to harm her.

Zahi Selim did not have that intent. He was focusing on charming her and getting her horizontal for other purposes entirely. It wasn't difficult to divine that even without checking his mental meanderings.

Somebody should tell him, for future reference, that he was trying too hard. He wouldn't need that tip in prison, where he would be very shortly if all went as planned tonight.

She gave up watching for Cameron's car lights and directed her attention to where they were going.

And promptly noticed they were now heading in the wrong direction.

"This is not the way to the marina," she said in what she hoped was a nonchalant but faintly reproving tone.

"I know," he said with a salacious smile.

Tess hid her frown behind the bored expression.

Did this little twerp think he could kidnap her or something? Definitely *something*. He was feeling pretty smug about it, too. She could sense that without even trying.

"You might tell me where you intend to go instead," she said, shifting impatiently in her seat. "You said I could trust you."

"Oh, but you *can!*" he protested. "Please don't be angry with me. I merely thought we might stop off at my place for a drink first. What do you say?"

"A drink? At your place?" she repeated, rolling her eyes. "Why didn't I see this coming?"

Tess felt her stomach flutter with apprehension. She really didn't want to have to disable him and ruin the plan they had to get him willingly onto the yacht.

She forced herself to remain calm, suddenly sensing that he had another reason for going to his house, one that had nothing to do with her. "It's quite presumptuous of you, but if you insist. I suppose I'm in no great hurry."

Tess knew she could handle this little dude on her worst day. One wrong move on his part and he'd be screaming for mercy, but she hoped it wouldn't come to that. She needed to see where he lived, find out where his computer was, didn't she? Here was the perfect opportunity, falling right in her lap.

They were leaving the commercial section and winding through tree-covered hills. No car lights were behind them. "Zee, where is this house you're taking me to? I like to know where I'm going."

"Not far. Relax, little Tessa. I promise you can trust me, and I will take you to the marina whenever you say. First, I have to do something important. Business, you see. Then we will enjoy a drink together."

"You don't consider *me* important?" she demanded, trying to sound kittenish.

"Well, of course you are! Have I told you how beautiful you look? Blue silk becomes you. And your hair…" He took a dangling curl between his fingers, leaned near and brought it to his lips.

This close, he smelled of garlic. *God's gift, indeed.* She moved away. Hard to get was not a bad way to play this, she decided.

"Where in London do you live?" she asked to distract him.

"Why do you ask? Do you know London well?"

"Of course. How long have you lived there? Did you attend school in England?" she asked, then realized she sounded too much like an interrogator, instead of a woman merely showing interest in a man. Immediately, she smiled sweetly at him and added, "I only ask because your English is so perfect."

Selim beamed and his chest puffed out. "I studied at Oxford."

"I thought as much," she replied, trying to hold the smile steady. She had almost blown it. "I suppose your business is based there. Otherwise you would live here, wouldn't you?"

"Tell me about yourself," he countered instead of answering.

Tess knew she had to manufacture a background and quick. "I was born in Toronto but have lived all over. My father owns…" She ducked her head as if suddenly shy. "Oh my, I've said too much. Father warned not to speak of the family or our circumstances unless I know someone very well."

He placed a hand on her arm and squeezed. "Wealth makes you vulnerable. I understand why that would bother him." He sat back, holding her hand in his. "I have a flat in Twickenham, but I will be moving soon."

"Somewhere here on the Côte d'Azur, I suppose," she said. "I can't imagine a better place to live. The nightlife is so exciting."

"Especially tonight." He smiled again and gestured in the direction the cab was going. "There, the villa just up ahead is where I stay."

When they arrived, he paid the driver and got out, holding the door for her and offering his hand.

Tess took it and stared after the cab as it drove away. "You've let him go. How will I get to the marina?" she asked. He was clearly thinking she wouldn't need any transportation once he persuaded her to stay the night. Fat chance of *that*.

"We're on the bay. I'll take you around in my boat."

Ah, he had a boat. Maybe that *was* him they had seen on the beach.

The so-called villa was small and not all that impressive considering the location. The red-tiled roof was low-slung, the facade rather plain, and the entry had been left unadorned. It looked uninhabited, like a house for rent.

When he guided her inside and turned on the lights, she was even less impressed. The furnishings were modern and sparse. No plants or anything colorful. She'd seen more interesting motel rooms. Again, she thought of a furnished rental property.

"Bachelor accommodations, they are all the same," she commented with a dismissive flap of her hand.

"As I said before, I'm house-sitting. The owner has no taste."

"There's an understatement." She didn't have to work very hard at projecting a rich girl's ennui. She followed him to the kitchen and watched idly as he poured them both a glass of wine.

He drank his down like medicine. "If you will excuse me for a few moments, I have to take care of something on the computer. Please, make yourself at home. Have more wine. I'll be right back."

She let him leave, then followed, moving languidly back into the living room and noting the only closed door leading off of it. She wandered closer, heard the tapping of a keyboard and then crossed the room again so she wouldn't be overheard when she talked to Cameron.

With the phone to her ear, she demanded in a whisper, "Where the heck are you?"

"Right outside," Cameron announced. "Are you okay?"

"Fine. We're going to the marina on his boat. Be on the yacht when we get there, and I'll get him on board somehow. I think he's sending another message now, as we speak. About that guy at the club—"

"Yeah, about him. Send that photo you took to Mercier first chance you get and request an ID." She jumped when the door opened and Selim appeared. "No!" she exclaimed into the phone. "You're to do as I said, Fabio! And do *not* bring anyone aboard with you, do you hear? And if I have a guest, I want you topside, at the wheel, with no interruption. *Capisce?*" She pretended to click the phone off and shook her head as if exasperated by the whole conversation.

"Problem?" Selim asked.

She smiled sweetly. "Not at all. You simply have to be firm with the help, or they will take advantage." She finished her wine and handed him the empty glass as he approached. "Could we go now? I have a bottle of Dom Pérignon and some divine beluga waiting on the *Jezebel*. Like to share?"

"Sounds lovely," he said. "This way." He led her back through the kitchen to the back door. "I'm sure my little runabout is not fancy enough for you, but it will get us there in no time."

"Wait!" *Too much of a hurry,* she thought. Cameron needed time to get there first. She ran a hand down Selim's arm when he stopped in his tracks. "Forgive me. I'm being a real boor, Zee. Why don't we have one more glass of wine here before we go? And I would love to see the rest of the villa."

He seemed confused by her sudden change in attitude, but he shrugged. "If you like."

"Here. I'll even pour," she offered, turning to the counter where he'd left the wine. She took time to examine the label. "Not a bad white really. Rather sweet but I like it."

He preened. "I chose it myself. I'm afraid I have a taste for sweets." His fingers traveled up her arm to her shoulder, and he flipped her earring with the tip of one finger. "Sweets such as you, *ma cherie*."

No need to read his mind to know what his intent was

at the moment. She laughed and proceeded to fill their glasses. "Well, then, a toast," she said, handing him his drink and practicing her eyelash batting. "To new friends and gorgeous surroundings."

"Hear, hear!" He clinked his glass to hers and took a sip.

"The villa? May I see the rest of it?"

He nodded. "Of course. This way."

They walked back through the nondescript living room to the open door leading off of it. He flipped on a light switch. "My bedroom," he said as she peered through the doorway.

The room was as nondescript as the rest of the place. It contained a double bed with a rumpled beige duvet, a lime green chair and a cheap-looking armoire. No way was she setting foot in there.

She backed away and headed for the other room. "So what is this? Guest quarters?" She opened the door herself and looked inside.

"The office," he replied.

She sensed anxiety. No wonder.

This was a much smaller room, outfitted with a futon, a straight chair and a simple desk holding a lamp and a laptop. He had turned the laptop off and closed it, she noted. Was that the famous instrument he used to threaten half a country?

"You must not do much work here," she said with a smile and a shrug. "One would expect something more elaborate for conducting a business."

"I am not a businessman as such," he admitted. "I am more of a consultant, one might say."

"Ah, I see." Tess backed out of the room. "Is that all there is here?"

"Except for the terrace out back and the gardens. That way leads down to the private dock. Are you ready?"

He seemed eager to leave. Or maybe eager to get to her yacht and consume that champagne and caviar she had mentioned. And her, too, of course.

"I'm ready," she said.

"For anything?" he asked. Then he grabbed her by the shoulders and kissed her soundly on the mouth.

Tess fought the urge to knee him and break his nose. Instead, she kissed him back, then pulled away, laughing. "I can see this is going to be a wild night in Tropez!"

"You know it, *bebe!*"

He took her hand and led her outside, closing the door behind her. She noticed he had left the lights on inside and started to question that, but decided that the rich wouldn't worry about anything as paltry as the electric bill.

He kept an arm around her as they descended the steps that led down to the dock. She saw his boat bobbing gently. It was a motor craft, not more than fifteen feet long. Similar to the one they had seen the man on the beach use earlier, if not the very same one. Tess wished they had caught him then.

She prayed Cameron would already be on the *Jezebel*, waiting for them. Not that she couldn't handle Selim herself, but she wanted to get this over with.

Suddenly an arm locked around her neck and jerked her away from Selim. Tess reacted automatically, kicking the assailant's knee with her heel and bending forward, but he stood firm, choking off her airway.

She had dropped her phone when he grabbed her, but hoped Cameron was still listening in and could hear the scuffle. "Let…me…go!" she screeched. Tess tried everything she knew to break the hold, but he was well trained. And very strong.

"Stop!" Selim cried, leaping to her defense and beating at the man with his fists.

"Shut up, you fool! She was watching you in the club. She followed. You know what that means." The guttural voice matched the roughness with which the assailant handled her.

Another man, the one Selim had met with in the club, approached then, and Tess stopped fighting. She was outmatched in strength, and this new guy had a weapon. Best to play meek until she could figure a way out of this. Men underestimating her had always proved her most effective weapon.

"Get her back inside," the second man ordered. "Selim, there will be a penalty for trying to evade us. You know that." He held a gun on Selim.

"She's just a girl I met. We were going to have drinks and party a little. Let her go. I already did what I was told to do," replied Selim.

The man shook his head. "The woman is here to find you. We must deal with her and change your location." He motioned for Selim to precede him back up the steps to the villa. Strong-arm still had her in a choke hold and pushed her along behind the other two.

Tess focused on keeping her feet on the ground, no small task when she was nearly lifted off them with every step. Release came so quickly, she fell to her knees.

Sucking in a deep breath, she wheeled around to attack, but saw her attacker tumbling down the stone steps to the landing.

A shot rang out. Selim dashed across the terrace as two men near Tess struggled over the gun.

She recognized Cameron immediately and trusted he would prevail. She kicked off her shoes, took off after Selim and tackled him just as he rounded the side of the villa.

She heard another shot and prayed Cameron was on top of things. *She* was. The tight-fitting dress had ripped up one side, baring her leg nearly to her waist. She straddled Selim's back, bent one of his arms behind him and was reaching for the other when Cameron arrived to help.

"You okay, Tess?" he demanded.

"Super," she gasped, getting her breath back.

"Get up off of him. If he runs, I'll kill him. You hear that, Selim?"

Selim nodded frantically. He was hyperventilating, and when he rolled over, Tess saw he was weeping.

"Get up," Cameron ordered. "We've got to get rid of those two in case someone heard the shots." He handed Tess a nine millimeter. "Shoot him if he runs again. One more shot won't matter that much."

She motioned for Selim to follow Cameron as they returned to the steps. The white-haired man lay staring at the night sky, his features ghostly in the moonlight.

Selim gasped. "Is he…"

"Dead as a mackerel," Cameron muttered as he hurried down the steps and knelt to check the other one.

Tess followed, pushing Selim along in front of her.

"This one's done for, too," Cameron said. "Let's dump them in the bay. We'll be long gone before they're found."

"You can't do that!" Tess exclaimed.

"Right by myself if I have to, but I'd appreciate some help. Selim, get over here and give me a hand."

"No! I cannot!" Selim thundered.

"Shoot him, Tess."

Chapter 9

"Wait!" Selim cried, throwing up his hands. "I'll do it."

Tess huffed out a breath she hadn't realized she was holding. Things were moving too fast. This wasn't right. She knew she ought to protest again, but couldn't think of an alternative plan. Cameron looked perfectly calm and in control, as if he'd done this sort of thing before. Had he?

Good as his word, Selim rushed to take the man's feet. Cameron lifted the man by his hefty shoulders, and they carried the body between them to the dock.

"Swing him a couple of times so he won't get tangled up in the pilings," Cameron ordered.

Selim complied.

Tess took the opportunity to locate her cell phone and recover her shoes. She quickly texted Mercier and sent him the photo of the man, now dead, that she'd taken in the club. She didn't explain all that had happened. There would be time for that aboard the yacht.

They had just dumped a body in the bay! How was she supposed to word that when she reported it?

"Now the other one." Cameron took the steps two at a time, and Selim scrambled to follow. As soon as they had dispatched White Hair, Cameron motioned them back to the villa.

Tess had to admit she was impressed in spite of the fact that she disapproved of the disposal of the bodies.

Cameron paused as they entered the doorway, and cradled her neck with his hand. "How's the windpipe?"

She touched the back of his hand and rasped, "No real damage. You all right?"

He winced. "Yeah, a little shook up. Didn't realize I was that out of shape. Haven't done any hand-to-hand in a while."

"You did fine," she said. He'd done better than fine. She'd probably be dead by now if he hadn't shown up when he did and if he hadn't done what he'd done.

Selim was leaning over the sink in the kitchen, being sick. Tess almost felt sorry for him. He had pleaded for her life and had actually tried to get Strong-arm to free her.

Cameron raised his eyebrows and sighed loud and long. "Well, this screws with Plan A. You guard the pip-squeak while I get his computer. We'll drive back to the marina and get him on board. If you have to shoot him, go for the knees. I want him alive until I find out who's running him."

"I will go with you," Selim said, wiping his mouth with a dish towel. "I cannot stay here."

"Definitely not an option," Cameron assured him and strolled on into the living room, leaving Tess to do as ordered.

She pointed with the gun and Selim followed Cameron.

In a few moments Cameron came out of the office with Selim's cased laptop, the webbed strap slung over one shoulder.

Selim groaned when he saw it but didn't offer any other protest. Tess felt his sense of futility and apprehension. She was a little apprehensive herself.

She had aided the other agents on cases before, but this was the first time she had actually participated in the capture of a felon. So far this collar had been extremely unorthodox. Cameron was unorthodox, to say the very least.

She wondered what Selim's interrogation would be like and how Cameron would go about it.

They were soon on their way in the Mercedes, which Cameron had parked down the drive when he had followed them in. Tess rode in the backseat with Selim, the weapon still trained on him. He appeared perfectly willing to go with them, but she would have employed the same trick herself until an opportunity to escape presented itself.

When they reached the marina, Cameron got out first, opened Tess's door and held out his hand. "Give me the gun. It will be in my pocket, trained on you, Selim. You'd better pretend to be happy about boarding." Then Cameron looked at Tess. "Your dress is ripped up the side, and your hair's a mess. Sure you're okay?"

"I'm sure." No point admitting how unsteady she felt and that the two glasses of wine had nothing to do with it.

She removed the hairpins, combed through her hair with her fingers and straightened herself up as best she could.

They proceeded to the marina and boarded without any problems. There were other people partying on the boats nearby. Two guys waved from the deck of one docked nearest the *Jezebel*. Tess smiled and waved back.

Cameron pushed Selim down onto the lounge in the saloon as soon as they were below deck. "We know you are involved in the threat to shut down the power grid on the East Coast of America. Will you cooperate and answer our questions truthfully?"

Selim shook his head, avoiding looking at either one of them. "I do not understand any of this. You have the wrong person."

"I have your computer and enough evidence on it and from other sources to earn you a death sentence for terrorism," Cameron responded. "Unless you help us by naming any coconspirators and details of plans and methods to be used by yourself or by anyone else."

"I know American law. You have to give me rights," Selim said, but with more fear than defiance in his voice.

"You'll soon see what *my* rights as a mercenary are. I make my own since I'm not bound by any oaths," Cameron said, his tone ominous.

He locked Selim in the forward cabin, warned him to keep quiet or face the consequences, and went directly to the bar.

Tess noted that Cameron had reversed the handle mechanism on the forward cabin door so that it locked from the outside, rather than from within. When had he done that? Talk about prepared. He had thought of everything.

He poured two shots of brandy and handed one to Tess. "Here, settle your nerves. It'll be good for your throat, too."

"You know I should have read him his rights. Anything you get out of him won't be admissible in court after that threat."

"I'm not interested in any future court case, damn it! I want the person who got him into this and anyone else they've hired besides Selim. I won't get that playing by the rules and neither will you."

Tess nodded. She noticed her hand was shaking as she took the glass from him.

He traced her neck with one finger and squinted. "Probably bruise up by morning," he muttered. "Sorry I took so long to get to you. I was inside, looking for evidence, when I heard the attack."

"Thank God you were still around," she said, taking a sip of the brandy, feeling the burn as it coated her throat. "I thought you'd be on your way back here."

He smiled. "I figured you could handle the boy until I got aboard, but I would have been right behind you."

"I'm sorry you had to kill," she murmured, taking another swallow, feeling the slow burn as it went down.

"The beefy one crushed his skull on the steps as he fell. All I did was box his ears to make him release you and yank the back of his coat to make him fall. The other one went down hard, though. Had me going for a minute there."

"Are you all right with it?" she asked, concerned but also curious. She had never had to use ultimate force and wondered if she would be as complacent about it as Cameron seemed to be. "It was you or him."

He nodded and tossed back his own brandy. "It was him or both of us, so no regrets."

"Thank you, Cameron," she whispered.

"No problem," he replied, sliding his hand to the back of her neck and kissing her gently.

Tess realized all she had been missing. Had she been overcompensating for her parents' lack of rules all these years?

When had her hands slid inside his jacket and embraced him? His body felt taut and hot beneath her palms. He moved against her, and she responded eagerly, with no hesitation. Hadn't she decided not to do this again? Where was her resolve? Did agents normally behave this way on assignment?

It was so hard to know what was normal. Or if she even wanted to be normal. This felt so good, so right. At least it did at the moment. She sighed when he broke the kiss and nuzzled her ear, so overwhelmed she almost missed what he was saying.

"I was afraid I'd lose you, Tess," he whispered. "Terrified."

Tess closed her eyes and found his mouth again, seeking the pleasure she had denied herself for so long. He groaned and lifted her off her feet, their bodies still locked in a full-length kiss. She vaguely resisted when he released her and led her to the master cabin.

"Let's get you out of that dress," he said, raking it off her shoulders.

She didn't care what his motives were at the moment. It didn't matter that they were on a mission, that a perp was on board who needed questioning. Nothing mattered but how his hands felt on her, how the silk slithered off her like a false skin of propriety and how desire welled up inside her to obliterate everything else in her mind.

"My God, your knees!" he exclaimed.

For a second, Tess thought it was a lusty compliment, but he pushed her back onto the berth and began examining them in earnest.

The cold rush of reason returned. She was sitting on the mattress, a puddle of blue silk around her ankles, wearing nothing but a demi bra, a thong, killer shoes and a fake tan. "What?" she gasped, crossing her arms over her chest.

"You've wrecked your knees, and they're still bleeding," he said as he stood up. "I'll get the first-aid kit."

She wanted to scream. Did the man have superhuman control, or what? How did he turn it off like that? Her entire body was quaking, and he looked cool as a cucumber.

She stared at his crotch and groaned at the mental analogy. Quite a cucumber it was, too. Maybe he couldn't turn it off entirely.

A deep breath or two and she accepted the inevitable. He had lapsed into doctor mode. Unfortunately, it wasn't to be the sort of playing doctor she wished for at that moment. "For the best. It's for the best," she muttered to herself.

He disappeared to get the kit, and she knew she ought to retrieve a robe or something. Modesty didn't seem all that critical, though, so she stayed right where she was until he returned.

Cameron stopped in the doorway, holding a large plastic box by the handle. "You look a little shocky," he muttered. "Better get you warmed up."

"I *was* getting pretty warm," she admitted with a wry laugh. She reached back to gather the lightly quilted bedspread and drag it over her shoulders. Maybe, just maybe, she was more in control than he was. "There. Better?"

He set down the first-aid kit beside her feet and went into the head. In a moment he returned with a wet cloth and towel.

"You want me to do that?" she asked politely.

"No. I can see better how to clean them up than you can. Just sit back and relax."

Yeah, right. Relax. But she did as he ordered and liked it, too. She couldn't remember a time when anyone had taken care of her, worried about skinned knees and whether she was warm enough. It felt almost as good as having him want her. But not quite.

Tess knew they would make love again; she was certain of it. And she wouldn't let the old Tess talk her out of it, either.

Apparently, Cameron was the one with the reservations now, using any old excuse to back out. Maybe he felt he had created something he couldn't control.

Maybe he had.

Cameron tended her scraped knees, cleaning and applying ointment and Band-Aids where they were needed. The scratches weren't actually that bad, but the sight of her bleeding even a little bit had sobered him immediately.

Tess was a virtual innocent, not a seasoned partner he could fool around with and forget as soon as the op was over. And what about the fact that he was already so involved he couldn't forget her even if he tried? She would expect some kind of continuing relationship, he was already halfway convinced he should offer that, and he couldn't afford to.

She didn't need a washed-up operative whose best deal from here on out would probably be fishing for a living. He didn't put much stock in the job offer from Mercier. Tess would go far in intelligence once she made her bones and got a little experience under her belt. So far, she'd done well, much better than he'd expected. He knew, of course, that Mercier would never have sent her in the first place if she didn't have what it took.

He wouldn't have sent her alone, either, and Cameron was well aware of that now. Mercier had selected him as a tool for teaching Tess the ropes in the field. This assignment, while crucial, shouldn't have proved as dangerous as it had. No one had counted on armed goons shadowing the hacker. Selim should have felt perfectly secure.

Maybe whoever had hired him hadn't trusted him. At any rate, the man in charge would probably get a little antsy if he knew Selim was running around unsupervised. That ramped up the urgency to get this job completed.

"There. All done," he said, allowing himself one last caress of Tess's slender leg. "We need to get under way."

She still had that slumberous look in her eyes. A look he had put there. He felt guilty leaving her unsatisfied, but less guilty than he'd feel if he did what they both wanted right now. Business had to come first.

"Get dressed. We'll anchor somewhere out in the

Mediterranean. No point going with the original plan now if we can get Selim to cooperate. We'll just go to Nice and fly out once I get the info we need."

"You aren't going to torture it out of him, are you?" she asked. "You know that's not allowed."

"I don't think I'll need torture," Cameron replied. "He's weaker than I thought, a real crybaby. It won't take much to break him."

"In his defense, he did try to save me," Tess said, looking up at him with mascara-smudged eyes. "Let me talk to him first. I think I can turn him."

"Yeah, into a slavering idiot, no doubt," Cameron said with an eye roll. "Okay, you can give it a shot. What we need is the name and location of his control. Get that and I'll be happy."

"I'll get it," she said with a determined nod.

"Sure you aren't sweet on the boy?" Cameron asked as he closed up the first-aid kit and avoided her eyes. She was getting to him. He didn't doubt the effect she'd have on Selim. "We can't afford sympathy at this point."

"Get real. I'm not that soft."

Cameron would argue that, but he didn't. "Okay, be ready when we anchor. Keep in mind we have to do whatever works. This is not a misdemeanor they were planning, and don't assume we've stopped it by getting our hands on Selim. People could die if the threat's accomplished, and Selim might not be the only one who can put it into motion."

"Duly noted." She sounded miffed that he didn't trust her. He did but needed to put some space and professional attitude between them right now.

He left her then and went to ready the boat to head out from Saint-Tropez. They needed to get out of sight of land so Selim would feel totally isolated with his interrogators and realize he had no hope of escape.

This was not Cameron's favorite part of the job, but it was certainly the most critical in this case. For now, however, he would let himself simply enjoy piloting the *Jezebel*. He took his pleasures where he could, and the master cabin was not the appropriate place today.

Tess washed her face, reapplied her makeup and did what she could to fix her hair. She put on a V-necked tank top, its appeal vastly improved by the push-up bra. She added a pair of drawstring pants that covered her skinned knees while baring her newly tanned midriff.

She still felt sexy, even in her own clothes, and readily admitted to herself that she wasn't dressing to wow Zahi Selim. Must be the heavy dose of lust involving Cameron and the aftermath of her empowering ruse as a wealthy playgirl. Her reflection smiled back at her. "All in the attitude," she muttered to herself.

She kept busy in the saloon, on her laptop, until Cameron dropped anchor and came below. He went directly to Selim's computer. Tess hadn't touched it since Cameron was the real expert.

After a few minutes, he abandoned the effort to access any of the files. "Protected, just as I figured it would be," he muttered. "We'll need his password. Handle it. I have a program to work through it, but that could take hours. We need him to tell us."

"Okay. We just had a transmission from Mercier.

The white-haired guy was Paul-Henri Junot, a mercenary, French, worked independently, no known affiliations. I should have gotten a photo of the other one, but you already had him in the water by the time I found my phone."

"He was just hired muscle, too. You ready to quiz Selim?"

"Whenever you are."

"Have you ever done this before? For real, I mean, not just in training?" he asked.

"First time for everything," she replied. "Bring him on."

Cameron nodded and went to unlock the door to the forward cabin. Tess waited in the lounge area of the saloon.

Selim kept a watchful eye on Cameron as they came in. He glanced at Tess, and she could sense, as well as see, his fear.

"Sit down, Zee," she said. "Would you like a drink?"

Selim shook his head, sat down on the lounge, where she indicated, and folded his arms over his chest, his chin nearly touching it.

"As you might have guessed from Cochran's questions earlier, I'm with the American government, Zee," Tess revealed. "And we know you are the one who threatened to shut down the power grid. This is considered a terrorist act."

"I am no terrorist!" Selim exclaimed.

Tess tried to catch his eye. "You have stated you will cut off the power in a large portion of my country unless we bow to extortion. Perhaps whoever hired you to make these threats against us is the terrorist."

"I am not a terrorist, and I don't know anyone who is," Selim declared. His movements became fidgety, and he refused to meet her eyes. "I would never hurt anyone or destroy anything."

She picked up on his mounting uncertainty and the gist of his actual thoughts. Should he reveal everything, or should he call the bluff? Was it a bluff? How much did they actually have on him?

Tess sighed. "You threatened to do just that. We have the proof, Zahi. It will go much better for you if you cooperate and give us the name."

Selim sniffed and stared at his feet.

She tried again. "Perhaps you didn't realize the harm this could cause when you agreed to do it, the disruption to our economy and the lives that would be lost," she said calmly.

Selim simply shrugged, but obviously her words troubled him.

Tess persisted. There was good in this young man; she knew it and pressed to reveal it. "Do you realize that nuclear reactors would stop functioning? Supplies for drinking water are controlled by electric pumps. Air travel depends on controllers having power to direct the flights. Rail service would stop. Last time the power failed, there were so many fires. People died, residents and firefighters. And think of the sick in outlying areas whose ability to breathe is dependent on the electric power available. Generators fail, Selim. They're not always reliable. What about the little babies on oxygen support in hospitals and clinics? They would be vulnerable."

"I have nothing to say to you," Selim mumbled, but he was weakening.

"You tried to save my life back at the villa, Zee," she reminded him. "I don't believe you're bad at heart. I will try to save your life if you help us get the one responsible for planning this."

"Save my life?" Selim jumped up from the lounge, pounded his chest with his fist and stuck out his chin in defiance. "I have harmed no one! Not one person. Do you think I am stupid because you were able to trick me? Your government will never give me a death sentence for posting a few e-mail messages that have come to nothing!"

Cameron grabbed him. "You're absolutely right, but I will. If you won't talk, you're worth nothing." He half carried, half dragged Selim to the railing and pushed him over, grabbing his ankles as he fell.

Chapter 10

Selim's shrill scream strangled on a sob.

"A name or a swim?" Cameron shouted down to him. "It's forty miles to shore."

"Help! Tessa!" Selim yelled.

She peered over the rail and shot Cameron a look of exasperation. "Pull him up, Cochran! You can't do this! It's against the Geneva convention and every other directive regarding prisoners!"

"I'm not a soldier, not even one of your agents. I haven't accepted one red cent or signed anything from the government for this operation."

Tess stamped her foot and shook her fist at him. "Bring him aboard, Cochran! That's an order!"

Instead, Cameron let go of one foot.

Selim screamed again. This time a name.

"What did he say?" Cameron asked. "Did you get that?"

Tess shook her head and sighed. "Cameron, bring him back up. He'll talk now."

Cameron smiled and managed to grasp Selim's flailing foot. "Okay, but this is his last chance." He hauled him in. "You hear me, Selim? Last chance."

Disheveled and gasping for breath, Selim collapsed on the deck. He looked up in abject terror. "He will kill me if I tell."

"I will kill you if you don't," Cameron assured him. "Get up and go back inside. I want a name. I want a location. And I want your password. You have three minutes after you sit down to tell me, or we're coming back out here, and I swear I'll throw you in, along with a bucket of chum to attract the sharks."

Selim was nodding rapidly as he scrambled to his feet and scurried back down to the relative safety of the saloon. Tess wondered how Selim's lawyers would spin this. How *she* would spin it when she did her report.

Cameron pushed Selim onto the lounge and stood over him, stance wide and hands on his hips. "Let's be real clear about this. We are not on American turf, and I don't work for the government. I'm just a pissed-off private citizen along for the ride, so don't count on me following any rules of conduct with regard to your capture. Give us the information and do it now."

Selim swallowed hard and nodded.

Tess stood by, totally noncommittal. Cochran was getting results; she had to give him that. She waited for him to stand back, then took a seat next to Selim.

She had sensed before that he felt most troubled by his actions causing people to die, so she concentrated on that.

"Now you listen to me," she ordered. "I'm telling you that what you were contracted to do will be deadly for a lot of people, Zahi. There are over two million men, women and children on power-dependent machines that only last a few hours at most without recharging."

"Two million?" Selim whispered, shaking his head.

Tess nodded. "Yes. They would be at risk when their oxygen-producing machines have the power cut. Those who are fully encased in iron lungs depend on power to keep them alive. Generators fail all the time. Batteries die after a few hours' use. And you would be personally responsible for all those people dying if you carried out your threat or allowed the man who hired you to do it. You don't want that on your conscience, do you? How would you live with yourself?"

Selim's confusion was clearing, his terror diminishing. His dark eyes sought hers. Tears rolled down his cheeks, and Tess knew they weren't entirely a result of fear for himself. He did have a heart. Youth, thoughtlessness and greed had blinded him, but now he had begun to understand that.

"So give us the information we need to stop this and prevent it from happening. Please," she added.

Selim looked at Cameron, since he posed the biggest threat. "We met only once, face-to-face, two years ago in London. Of course, he would not give me his real name, but I discovered it."

"Let me guess," Cameron said. "You sneaked a photo of him and hacked into our driver's license database."

Selim shrugged one shoulder, an admission. "He is Jason Bulgar. I suspected his plan had to do with more than the money, that perhaps he had worked for the Department of Energy, because he knew so much about it. He had advertised for a computer expert. I was pretty good. I needed the money, so I contacted him."

"Were there others who answered?" Tess asked.

"Yes, but he said he chose me because I was the best," said Selim. "I confessed to him I could hack into any system when he hinted that was what he needed done."

Cameron huffed. "I don't think we can count on the supposition that you were the only one he hired. There might be others, whom he has kept in reserve and could call on."

Selim knitted his brows. "I don't think so. He would have used them later instead of looking me up, since I had been caught before, don't you think? Maybe he trusted me because I did not try to involve him then."

"Trusted you? Did he know that you knew his real name?" quizzed Tess.

Selim shook his head. "No. He still does not know that."

"How much did he pay you this time?" Cameron asked.

"He gave me only five thousand in advance for expenses and promised me ten percent of the take when your government paid," Selim revealed. "I did everything he asked the last time, so he said he trusted me."

"I knew it had to be an insider!" Cameron exclaimed, pounding his palm with his fist. "Where is he now?"

"I don't know. Honestly, I don't, and I didn't try to find out." Selim shook his head and cast a worried glance up at Cameron. "He contacted me through e-mail this time. I found out only this past week that he had those two men following me."

"Did he say why?" Tess asked.

"For my protection," Selim said. "I told him I would send the messages to the Department of Energy for him as he asked. If the responses were negative and they wouldn't agree to pay, I would shut down the grid when he ordered me to do it."

"How would you have gained access?" Tess asked.

"Simple enough, really. Power-generating and power-distributing companies are connected through the Internet, and the control software they run is available if you know how to get it," Selim explained.

"Are you the one who hacked into the system last time?" asked Cameron.

Selim sighed, sniffed and sat back in defeat. "No, it was not necessary. He had the codes and passwords to get into the programs controlling the grid. All he wanted was for me to send the messages."

"They change those codes regularly," Cameron said. "He has to be the one who wrote the program to do it, or he's in control of whoever did. That's the only way. Maybe before he left, he hid a code that transmits to him whenever they change them."

"Then why doesn't he do the shutdown himself if he's that savvy?" Tess asked. "Have you thought about that, Zee? Did you consider that maybe you were hired to be the fall guy?"

"The what?" Selim asked, wide-eyed.

"The scapegoat," Cameron said. "The one who would

be held responsible. Once you did what he wanted, he would have arranged to get rid of you, maybe a suicide setup with a note on your computer, confessing everything. You wouldn't be allowed to live or be captured again."

"But I did nothing to implicate anyone else the last time!" Selim argued. "He wouldn't have me killed!"

"You didn't admit to an accomplice then, because there was no proof of your involvement, and you knew they would have to let you go. This time he had you guarded so you wouldn't be caught alive again, as you were in London. Even if he thought you couldn't give his name, you have seen him and would be able to identify him."

Selim leaned forward and buried his face in his hands.

"I need to access your computer. What's your password?" Cameron prodded.

"Moneyforme," Selim answered readily. "I have been so stupid! I can't believe how stupid."

Tess shot Cameron a warning look to ease up as she spoke to Selim. "But you have the chance now to fix this, Zahi. You can save all those people and put Bulgar out of commission. Will you help?"

Selim uncovered his face and took a deep breath. "Any way that I can. What would you have me do?"

"See if we can track his e-mails to the source and find out where he is. We could go through the NSA and have it done, but speed is essential. Can you do it?" Cameron asked.

Selim shrugged. "Of course. Child's play."

"Do it then." Cameron gave him the laptop brought

from the villa. As he did so, he said to Tess, "Call in the name. Get what they have on Bulgar. They will have checked all present and former employees first thing, so it should be compiled already."

Selim logged on as Cameron observed. "Don't even think about trying to warn him," Cameron said, his tone deadly.

"Why would I do that?" Selim asked. "If I help you, then you will help me. Is that right? You will promise?"

Tess answered. "I'll still have to arrest you for conspiracy, Zee, but I'll certainly ask for leniency and do whatever I can. You do understand that I can't just let you go?"

Selim considered that for a moment, and Tess could feel his apprehension and deep disappointment that his only hope of freedom and any kind of future had been dashed. She could also sense his determination to do the right thing in spite of that. Finally he nodded acceptance.

She smiled encouragement and gestured toward the computer. "I knew you'd do the right thing, Zee. Go ahead."

While Tess called Control and gave Bulgar's name and her request for information, Selim went to work, Cameron watching his every move. No trust there, but Selim had slipped out of the noose before. Maybe she should remember that and not count too heavily on her limited psychic ability sensing remorse. She still might be projecting what she wanted to sense from him, instead of picking up what he was really feeling.

Tess wondered how long she would be doing these sorts of missions before she gained confidence in her extrasensory perception. Would she ever be able to depend on it?

Very shortly, word came back on Bulgar's identity. "He was downsized three years ago," she told Cameron. "Took it hard but issued no threats that were recorded. He was eliminated as a suspect."

"Why?"

"They thought he was probably dead. He disappeared and stopped contact with family or friends after a couple of months. Apparently, he let a whole year pass and then decided to get revenge. Or maybe he thought he deserved huge compensation. Anyway, they're faxing his photo and employment records."

It took two hours for Selim to trace Bulgar's e-mails to a general location. He sat back and looked elated by his efforts. He had solved the puzzle, won the game, and Tess could feel his sense of pride.

"Well?" she prompted.

"He is on the island of Martinique. The trace ends at one of the two servers there. Sorry I can't give you an address, but he's there. At least he was as of the last message he sent to me," Selim announced.

Cameron studied the results. The e-mail had bounced around through a long routing string of servers all over the world. Finally, he nodded. "Perfect. We'll soon have him right where we want him."

"How do we do that?" Tess asked.

Cameron smiled. "We're flying to the Caribbean."

"To search Martinique," she said, guessing.

Cameron shook his head. "No, it could take us weeks to find him that way. He's going to come to us."

"We'll need backup," she said as she punched in Mercier's number and waited for him to answer.

"Get off the phone, Tess. No backup, or I'm off this mission," Cameron said. "That's how I got shafted last time."

"We might need the team. In fact, I'm not going in without them," she declared.

"You're on your own till they show up, then," Cameron replied with a determined set of his jaw. "I'll take you and Selim back to Nice, and you can take it from there."

He left the saloon and went above, leaving her alone with Selim and with Mercier's voice on the phone, demanding, "Tess? Tess, are you there? Is something wrong?"

"Sorry, sir, I was just calling to check on that photo of Bulgar," she said, her eyes still on the doorway through which Cameron had disappeared. The motor started, and the yacht began to move.

"Faxed it a few minutes ago along with his records," Mercier replied. "Anything else you need?"

She hesitated only a few seconds. "No, sir. Thanks."

Why didn't she given Mercier the plan they had for Bulgar and let him decide whether to send the team or not? She could still do that, but instead she closed the phone and looked at Selim. "Get back in the forward cabin now, Zee."

"There is no need to lock me away, Tessa. I promise to do precisely as you say."

"Promises are well and good, but business is business. Let's go."

When she had secured the prisoner, she went above to talk to Cameron. "I didn't call in the troops," she told him when she reached the bridge.

He nodded, his eyes on the sea ahead of them, as he slowed and cut the power. "Let's get below and proceed then."

He gave her no thanks for trusting him. No attagirl for turning Selim. Well, maybe Cameron was the one who had actually done that by dangling him over the side of the boat. At any rate, she had expected some measure of appreciation for her capitulation in the backup matter and got none.

Why was she still knocking herself out to please people, anyway? Why did she need someone else's praise and validation or thanks? Hadn't she learned anything by her struggle to excel and overcome her lackadaisical upbringing? She was pretty damn self-sufficient.

What she thought of herself as an agent and as a person was the only crucial opinion, the only one that ultimately counted.

That realization reminded her why she had never really needed a man around. *Who needs you, anyway, Cochran!*

The little voice in her head argued that she did, and that possibly she was mixing up validation with something else she needed even more than that.

Cameron sat down with the computer again and logged on to Selim's e-mail. Tess watched as he composed a message that was blackmail, pure and simple.

If Bulgar didn't meet face-to-face in St. Thomas the next morning at nine o'clock and produce another five thousand euros or the equivalent in U.S. dollars, Selim would contact the U.S. Department of Energy and reveal Bulgar's plan and his real identity. He signed with the letter Z as Zahi Selim had done in previous e-mails to Bulgar.

"Extorting the extorter. Could work," she said.

"It better. We won't wait for an answer. If he doesn't agree to meet Zahi in St. Thomas, then at least we'll be in the general area where we can go after him."

"Why St. Thomas?" she asked, then answered herself. "Oh, wait. Because it's under U.S. jurisdiction, and Martinique belongs to France! Brilliant."

"Thanks, if it works and he doesn't catch on. Britain owns some of the Virgin Islands, but St. Thomas is ours. Besides, I've been there before, and I like the idea of being on turf I know for something like this. Also, Bulgar will feel safer meeting in the islands than if he had to go to the mainland."

"I wonder if he owns that villa in Saint-Tropez," Tess said.

"Probably rented it for Zahi as part of the frame job. It looked like a rental, didn't you think?"

She laughed a little and ran a hand through her hair. "Well, I haven't actually seen that many villas, if you want the truth, but I did have the same thought. Can't fault the location, though. It's where an Egyptian playboy might roost."

"Sorry your first visit to the Côte d'Azur was so short," Cameron said. He settled back in his seat.

"Can't say it was uneventful, though."

Cameron closed the computer and put it back in its

case. "Well, we're on the homestretch now. Should wind this up tomorrow and be on our way to D.C."

Tess nodded. "I think Bulgar will come to St. Thomas, either to pay Zahi off or kill him. You're pretty big on offering bait, aren't you?"

"It usually works. It did with Selim. Why don't you work on him a little more before we dock?"

"Okay. What about his passport?"

"I have it, along with a work visa and his international driver's license. All his papers are in the zippered pocket of his laptop case. He probably kept them there for a quick getaway if he ever needed one."

She went to unlock the forward cabin and let Selim out, while Cameron went above, to the wheel, to continue their trip to Nice.

The private jet that had brought them to Nice was already back in the States, involved in another mission, so Cameron had to charter one to take them to the islands. He phoned Mercier for authorization to do so but offered no details of their plan. He reported only that they were following a strong lead to the individual who had orchestrated this threat.

The flight was taking longer than expected due to the weather. Once they were out over the Atlantic, it was necessary to detour around a storm that had formed off the African coast.

Tess sat across the aisle from Cameron and spent the time manning Selim's computer, alternately gathering Web info about the Virgin Islands to familiarize herself with the location and watching for an answer to the e-mail Cameron had sent to Bulgar.

Selim, in the window seat next to her, played solitaire with a deck of cards he'd found in the pocket on the back of the seat.

Cameron was using his own computer to write a detailed report of their trip, including the preparation for and apprehension of Zahi Selim.

He included the incident with the two men at the villa and their disposal. Might be some flack over that, but probably not. Investigations into the deaths of two known mercenaries wouldn't last more than a couple of days and would get nowhere. The authorities would figure good riddance and soon forget it.

He omitted the over-the-side tactic he had used during Selim's interrogation, stating only that the subject cooperated willingly. Tess could add to or correct that if she wanted to, but he didn't think she would. She had promised Selim she would speak for leniency on his behalf, and that would be more likely granted if he hadn't been coerced in any way to give information and help capture Bulgar.

The plane shuddered and Tess grabbed the armrests. "Man, I hate this turbulence!"

"Yeah, it's pretty rough. Hope this weather heads north," replied Cameron.

He went back to work. Reports were his least favorite task during or after an op, but he recognized the necessity and did them as quickly as possible. Tess would do hers, they would be debriefed separately after the mission and that would be that.

Would they really offer him a job if he was successful? Probably not. No way he could hold them to the promise with nothing in writing.

He'd been branded a rogue agent and blacklisted by the CIA, no small thing to get around. He didn't have any expectations with regard to that. The promise was probably empty and had almost surely been made in order to secure his help with this particular op. So be it. Back to the fishing and his life on Tybee.

Tess would go on to bigger and better things, he was sure. She had what it took, played things by the book.

Or did she? He'd been mighty surprised by her agreement not to call in a backup team. And she hadn't kicked up too much dust about his treatment of Selim or getting rid of those goons back in Saint-Tropez.

He had lied to Selim, of course. The acceptance of the badge and creds back on Tybee had committed him officially, and he certainly was working for the government. He had no doubt that he would be held responsible for the way he'd gotten the information out of Selim. Not that he cared, as long as Tess didn't take any heat for it. He'd see that she wouldn't.

He liked that she was flexible enough to tolerate a little rule breaking. She had offered a couple of token protests to his treatment of Selim, so she should be covered.

"Here it is!" she exclaimed. "Bulgar's response."

Chapter 11

Cameron crossed the aisle and crouched by Tess to read Bulgar's answer to the e-mail. Selim edged over to see it as well.

"He agreed to meet on St. Thomas and bring the money," Cameron muttered. "I guess that's that. When he does, we'll take him into custody. That should do it."

"He will kill me," Selim said with a dejected sigh.

"He would have to kill us first," Cameron assured him. "And you know that's not going to happen."

The turbulence grew worse, shaking them to the point where even Cameron felt uneasy. Then he felt the plane begin to climb. "We'll be okay. Pilot's getting above it. Relax."

"This might make me a white-knuckle flyer from

now on," Tess admitted, then issued a relieved sigh when the flight smoothed out.

A couple of hours later they descended and enjoyed a perfect landing. They had gained almost six hours even with the delay, so it was still daylight.

Customs took less than a half hour since they were traveling light, Tess flashed her badge and they had landed in between planes bearing tourists. Cameron went to the rental-car desk, signed the papers and got a key.

"I called ahead. We have a bungalow on the off side of the island. Better if we don't take this any more public than we have to," Cameron told Tess. "I'll e-mail Bulgar the location early in the morning. No point advertising where we are, or he might get creative tonight if he flies in early."

"You think he might already be here?" she asked.

"Well, he didn't have far to go," Cameron said.

They went to the car lot, and he punched the unlock button to locate their vehicle. Clouds rolled in quickly and rain began to fall. The storm they had flown around must have reached the islands. He hoped it would be over before morning.

They got in the Hyundai sedan, Tess in the back with Selim. "How in the world did you manage to get a place to stay on such short notice?" she asked.

"I know the owner," Cameron said over his shoulder. "He's making himself scarce for the duration, no questions asked. Called in a favor."

She shook her head. "Do you know somebody everywhere?"

"If I don't, I pretend to. This guy I do know, however.

We did some business together a while back. He's retired now."

"I take it you trust him?" Tess asked.

Cameron nodded. "As far as I need to. He will be gone when we get there, and won't come back until we leave. I promised him what the big hotels get, and he was happy with that. This is the storm season, and he said he might as well fly to the mainland for a couple of weeks' vacation."

"I can't imagine anyone needing a vacation from a Caribbean island," she replied.

"He said they were expecting bad weather in the next couple of days, and I guess he's right, since it's already started raining," said Cameron.

Tess nodded. "Well, I hate to see our expense total for this trip. Jack will croak."

Cameron didn't care. He admittedly hadn't economized on anything. If they wanted his services on this op, they could damn well make it worth his while. The actual pay probably wouldn't be that much.

Maybe he was after getting a little compensation, just like Bulgar intended, but at least Cameron's efforts were legal. Besides that, he figured Tess hadn't been many places in her short career, and he wanted her to enjoy it as much as possible in the limited time they had.

Or maybe, just maybe, you're trying to impress her, Mr. Big Shot, his conscience suggested. Cameron smiled. *Maybe so. You took your jollies where you could get 'em.*

He did want to impress her. He wanted to give her the time of her life, buy her fine wine, send her dozens of roses and make love to her on the beach. But they had made love once, and he figured that was about all he could expect or ought to try for.

Tess was the kind of woman men like him only dreamed about hooking up with. Actually having someone like her on a long-term basis was out of the question for him. He shouldn't even want long term.

By the time they reached the bungalow, it was fully dark and raining harder. Cameron went in first, checked it out, then beckoned Tess to enter with Selim.

"This is pretty posh for a one-night stay," she observed. Cameron could see she was pleased, however. "It's lovely, isn't it?"

"It's private enough for our purposes, too, and that's the important thing," he replied. "I guess we'd better eat, then get some sleep. Tomorrow's the big day."

They feasted on the frozen, prepackaged meals and bottled soda Cameron had requested the owner stock for them.

He regretted they hadn't been able to stop at a restaurant and sample the local cuisine, but felt it necessary to limit their time in public places. He still didn't trust Selim not to make a run for it.

Selim was nodding off before they finished eating. Cameron roused him and ordered him into the bedroom that had twin beds. He asked Tess for plastic restraints and cuffed one of Selim's wrists to the headboard. Then he lay down on the other bed and waited until Selim fell asleep before joining Tess in the living room.

"He's down for the count," he said as he took a seat to finish his soda. "You ready to turn in?"

"More than ready. Events are catching up with me. I want a long, hot shower and a good eight hours' sleep."

He stood when she did and reached out to clasp her shoulder. "I should have said it before, Tess, but you've done a great job. Played it just right."

"Thanks. I'd love to say the same about you, but I can't agree with your interrogation tactics. You didn't hurt him, but you did scare him to death."

Cameron smiled down at her. "I'm not a strong proponent of torture, but when time is short, you go with your instincts."

"He's on board with us now," she said with a decisive nod. "I know I'm reading him right."

"Reading him? His thoughts, you mean?"

"His mind's an open book. He never really thought things through before. To him, it was just a game. A profitable game, but that's how he saw it. He never figured that people would actually suffer and die if he cut the power. In a way, he was taunting what he viewed as a spoiled society, with its inability to get along without electricity."

Cameron huffed, unable to hide his amusement. "You got all that from the little he said? Actual words?"

"No, he doesn't think in English, or I probably could. He's a good subject for it," she said with a confident smile. "I could sense his emotions very clearly."

"I think in English." He looked deeply into her eyes. "Can you read my mind right now?"

She looked away, still wearing that smile. "Of course I can."

"No, you can't. If you could, you'd get all huffy and slap my face."

She looked up at him then, and he saw the dare in her expression. That was when he kissed her. To hell with the rules. Tess wanted this as much as he did. With a response like that, she had to.

He felt her arms slide around him, her hands grip his back, her breasts press against his chest and her lower body arch into his. Arousal zinged through him with the speed of light.

Just when he would have lifted her off her feet and carried her into that other bedroom, she pushed away. "We can't do this," she gasped. "Not right now and you know it."

He kept a grip on her waist. But she was right. They were on a crucial part of the mission, had a prisoner in the next room and needed to keep their minds on the next phase of the op.

He knew she was right, but the blood leaving his brain and pumping through his veins said otherwise. He backed off. *No means no,* he kept repeating in his mind. *No means no.*

"Good night, Cameron," she said, the words little more than a whisper. She patted his chest once with her palms, and then she was gone.

Cameron stood for a long time, waiting for his breathing to even out and his heart rate to subside to something approaching normal.

Oh, man, he was in so much trouble. It wasn't just sex on the beach he wanted with Tess.

Tess woke to the smell of coffee brewing. Her Timex said it was seven, a late morning for her. She got up, pulled on a pair of beige slacks and a matching shell. Today they'd be arresting Bulgar. She should abandon pretense and become an agent again with the proper looks and attitude.

She donned a short-sleeved brown linen jacket and sensible brown flats. *Pretty professional for an agent in the field,* she decided as she surveyed herself in the dresser mirror.

Her hair had lost its oomph, so she scooped it back into a low ponytail and wrapped that into a bun at her nape, securing it with a few hairpins. But she couldn't bring herself to go out there barefaced. She hurriedly added a minimum of makeup.

Would Cameron be disappointed that she had reverted to the old Tess? Well, she was who she was, after all, and it was time to end the fantasy all the way around.

"Hey, she's alive!" Cameron quipped, getting up from the kitchen table to pour her coffee for her. "Want some breakfast? Jerry's fridge is pretty well stocked for a bachelor's."

"One of those cinnamon buns will be fine," she said, reaching for the package that was already open. "Morning, Zee."

Selim nodded, looking and feeling pretty glum, she noted.

Cameron finished his coffee. "I'll e-mail Bulgar and have him meet Zahi here at nine. You and I will stay out of sight until he's inside. Should be an eventless bust if Zahi behaves himself and doesn't warn him off at the door." He shot their captive a warning look.

"I said I would not," Selim mumbled.

"You won't be sorry," Tess promised. "At least you'll be able to live with your conscience, right?"

Selim shrugged and nodded. "If he lets me live. What if he shoots me before you can do anything?"

"He won't," Cameron said. "He'll want to talk to you first, learn how you identified him and find out what happened to your watchdogs. We'll be ready to take him as soon as he gets here."

"Maybe he's actually coming to deal," Tess said. "He might be planning to pay you off and go on as planned."

Cameron agreed. "His reply indicated that. Somehow I don't think he's into physical force, not personally, anyway. The very nature of his plan proves that he prefers to exact revenge from a distance. Doesn't want to get his hands dirty."

Selim looked hopeful, desperately wanting to believe that Bulgar offered no immediate threat to him.

"It'll be okay, Zee," Tess said with a smile. "You are doing the right thing, you know."

Cameron had turned on the television in the living area, which was open to the kitchen. An announcer was giving the weather report, warning that continued rain and high winds were expected.

"Sounds like that disturbance we flew around blew this way instead of turning north, like they expected," Cameron said. "We'd better keep a close eye on the weather."

An hour later the announcer declared that the storm had indeed changed direction, picked up speed and increased to hurricane force. While it probably wouldn't make landfall on St. Thomas, it was entirely possible that it might. Residents were advised to prepare.

"What does that mean? Prepare?" Tess asked. "What do we do?" She remembered the devastation in New Orleans with Katrina years ago. "How do you get ready for something like that?"

"Seek shelter, but we'll have time to do that after the bust," said Cameron. "No way we can get off the island unless we abort the mission. We might as well do this and then worry about weathering the storm."

Tess knew he was right. They might not have another chance at Bulgar. Still, they could all die if they weren't prepared. "But what if—"

"The brunt of it is at least several hours away," Cameron said. "We'd better get in place in case Bulgar decides to come early. Tess, you remain in the bedroom at the front, and leave the door cracked a bit until he's well inside. If he tries to run for it when you come in and announce yourself, stay between him and the front entrance. I'll take the back, in case he goes that way."

"If he makes it back outside in this downpour, we could lose him," Tess noted. The landscape was hilly and forested, and the bungalow was fairly isolated on the inland side of one of the hills. Bulgar could hide out for days or maybe work down to the coast and escape by boat.

Cameron nodded. "Zahi, you answer the door when he gets here, then walk around behind the sofa, as you talk to him. When the collar goes down, drop behind the sofa just in case he has a weapon."

Selim swallowed hard, obviously headed for panic mode.

Cameron must have realized it, too. He clapped Selim on the shoulder. "Don't worry, kid. I know you can do this. We'll have it under control. Take a deep breath, and be a hero for once in your life, okay? Think of all the lives you'll be saving."

Selim straightened his hunched shoulders and stoked up his courage. He looked at Tess. "I trust you."

"Good man," she said with a smile. "Hang in there now, and don't show any nerves, okay?"

Selim gave her a decisive nod and returned the smile.

The wait seemed interminable. Tess's own nerves were about to snap when they heard a car engine through the driving rain. A car door slammed. Selim headed for the front door. Tess sensed his terror and hoped it didn't show on his face.

Selim opened the door at the first knock. "Come in," he said and stood back. Peeking out, Tess could see Selim quickly retreat behind the sofa as the other man entered.

Bulgar looked to be in fair shape, though older than he appeared in the photo Mercier had faxed. He was carrying a briefcase and had one hand in his pocket. If he had a gun in there, she didn't want him to have a chance to use it.

She swung the door open, grabbed him from behind and buckled his knees with hers. He dropped with a guttural cry, and she slammed him forward to the floor, landing on top of him.

The briefcase flew to one side, and his hand came out of his pocket with a pistol in it. She grabbed his wrist and dug into the pressure point with her thumbnail. The pistol tumbled out of his hand.

Cameron had rushed to help. He kicked the weapon aside and knelt to assist her, cuffing Bulgar with the plastic restraints she had given him earlier.

"There we go," Cameron said. He stood up and helped Tess to her feet. "Perfect takedown," he said to her, grinning with pride.

She sensed that his pride in her was real, and she had never felt so powerful and in control. "Thanks. I guess that's it, then."

Cameron read Bulgar the Miranda rights. "Do you understand?" he asked. He gave Bulgar a rough shake when the man remained silent. *"Answer!"*

"Lawyer," the man replied, breathless from exertion. "Nothing…till I get a lawyer."

"Fine by me. I wasn't looking for a long conversation." Cameron left him lying on his stomach, hands secured behind him.

Selim was on the floor behind the sofa, hands over his head.

"Okay, hero, you can get up now," Tess said. She and Cameron shared a wry grin.

"I did it. I did it," Selim kept saying.

"I guess we can worry about the weather now," Tess said, straightening her jacket and brushing a strand of hair off her brow.

"See what's on the news," Cameron suggested as he recovered Bulgar's weapon. "Looks like the storm's over in here."

The prisoner shot him a hate-filled glare.

Tess turned on the television, and the announcer sounded much more urgent than he had earlier.

"…miles per hour after changing direction and passing over warm currents, has now been classified a category two storm."

"A cat two? That's not sounding good," Cameron muttered. He went to the window and looked out. "Darkening up out there."

The announcer continued. "Landfall of the eye is expected at seven o'clock this evening on St. John. All air and marine traffic has been suspended for the duration, and residents are advised to take shelter as soon as possible. Remember the surprise Hurricane Marilyn gave us in nineteen ninety-five?"

"We are going to die!" Selim exclaimed, hands buried in his hair as he shook his head. "We have to get off the island!"

"Shut up, Zee, so we can hear the rest of this," Tess snapped.

The message sounded urgent. "St. John residents directly in the path have been evacuated by ferry to St. Thomas. Those of you here in St. Thomas, seek high ground if possible to escape flooding, and take immediate cover within the strongest structure available. I repeat, residents of the island, take immediate cover."

"What do you say?" she asked Cameron. "Should we commandeer a boat and try to outrun it?"

"And go where?" Cameron asked, worry lines marring his brow.

Chapter 12

"It's not safe to leave in any direction. I guess we're stuck on St. Thomas for a while," Cameron said. "But let's get closer to the airport and find a shelter if we can." He picked up the briefcase Bulgar had dropped. "Grab our laptops and Selim's. Leave the luggage."

He dragged the resisting Bulgar to his feet and gave Selim an order. "Selim, you help Tess with the computers."

They hurried out to the car. Tess got in back with Bulgar, and Selim sat in the passenger seat beside Cameron.

"Take this road to Charlotte Street and hang a left," Tess said as she studied the map. "The hospital is our best bet."

"And everyone will be headed there," Cameron argued.

"Okay, then one of the big hotels would probably

be better," she said just as Cameron slammed on the brakes.

"Tree across the road. And we haven't passed any side roads to detour," Cameron muttered. "We'll have to go back, dig in and hope to hell the house is as sound as it looks. At least it's on high ground."

"Maybe too high. We could get the brunt of the winds. Could we walk out from here?" she asked, leaning forward as if that would help to see. Palm trees were bowing, and things were beginning to fly around them, small objects, clumps of leaves.

"No way." Cameron slammed the car in reverse and backed up the road, his lips tight with apprehension. "I know the devastation a cat four or five can cause, and this is already a two. That could change rapidly, if it hasn't already."

So far, no big thing. Only a small category two hurricane, a couple of hours of harassment. But the expected 105-mile-per-hour winds could quickly turn into everyone's worst nightmare, and Tess knew it. Winds were already pummeling them, and the main force hadn't even hit yet.

They parked the car beside Bulgar's and rushed inside. Tess carried the briefcase and two laptops. Cameron held the one taken from Selim and dragged the silent Bulgar with his other hand. Selim stayed close to Tess, all but hugging her side, as if she could protect him.

"The walk-in closet in the master bedroom is probably the safest spot," Cameron said and went directly there, pushing Bulgar in one corner, stashing the computer and motioning for Tess to do the same with the other two. Selim followed and crouched in the corner opposite Bulgar.

It was a fairly large walk-in with coated wire shelving around the perimeter. A man's hanging clothes took up one side, and the other was stacked with books and small appliances, a dehumidifier, a space heater, plastic tackle boxes and such.

"Let's get rid of these," Cameron said and began lifting some things out and tossing them into the bedroom. "Tess, go and get pillows and blankets. And run us some water in whatever containers you can find."

"Some food, too!" Selim added, staying right where he was in the corner, beneath the shelves.

Tess and Cameron settled in with their captives, waiting for the storm to pass. Tess had left the television on with the volume maxed so they could hear any further reports. She had also found a battery-powered radio but was saving that in case the power went out.

Soon it sounded as if all hell was breaking loose. Objects were crashing onto the structure. Glass shattered, and Tess figured it was the French doors to the patio off the dining area.

The light in the closet blinked off, and the television fell silent. Cameron rustled around, and light soon flared from the Coleman lantern he had located before they had settled in.

"Can't run this for long, so look around you and memorize where everything is that you might need," he instructed.

When he turned the lantern off again, they sat silently,

listening to the devastation going on outside their cocoon, wondering whether it would remain secure.

The roof could go at any minute, Tess figured. Then the walls, along with the contents of the closet, including its inhabitants. Her heart pumped like crazy.

"My ears are popping," Selim complained.

"Barometric pressure's dropped," Cameron noted.

Tess turned on the radio. Nothing but static. She felt Cameron's hand grasp hers. He just held it. Maybe he needed the human contact.

She wished they were snuggled close, because she sure as hell needed it. As if he heard her thoughts, he shifted position and slipped an arm around her.

Bulgar still hadn't said anything. He sat on Cameron's opposite side.

Selim must have heard the movement, because he scrambled across the closet and pressed against Tess on the other side from Cameron. So there Tess and Cameron sat, flanked by their prisoners, waiting for the commotion to cease.

Tess took Selim's hand, the one that had landed on her outstretched leg. "We'll be okay," she declared. "Everybody just stay calm."

Cameron didn't offer any verbal reassurance, but he gave her shoulder a squeeze. So they sat silently on the cold tiled floor, huddled against a storm they heard but couldn't see. Imagination was a terrible thing, but the reality could prove worse, Tess thought.

Selim began muttering under his breath. She understood enough of it to recognize prayer. *No atheists in foxholes or a hurricane's eye,* she figured and mumbled a little prayer of her own. Cameron and Bulgar remained silent.

A horrible wrenching staccato clattered above them. Roof tiles giving it up. The wind increased its roar and the entire structure shook.

Eventually the loud whistling and the slap of debris abated a little, then stopped. The roof had held, at least the portion directly over their heads.

"It's over," Tess whispered.

"Half over maybe. We're probably in the eye," Cameron said with a sigh. He lit the lantern again and reached for a soda. "If either of you need a bathroom break, now's the time, and make it snappy. Tess first."

Cameron got up and opened the door. Debris was piled up outside it, so he kicked a path for her, then returned to the closet and closed the door to give her some privacy. Tess had expected devastation, but it was still a shock to see the mess that littered the floor.

Before returning to their shelter, she peeked into the other rooms. Water had dashed inside the broken windows, along with muddy unidentifiable objects, leaves and branches. The furniture was intact, but soaked and probably ruined. She went back to the relative comfort of the closet and sat down, knowing the respite could be of short duration.

Cameron accompanied Selim to the bathroom, still not trusting enough to leave him alone. Then he did the same with Bulgar. The wind still had not picked up again when they resumed their places. They waited until four o'clock in the afternoon.

The expected second and worse phase never hit. Tess slept a little, since it was dark as pitch and there was nothing else they could do.

Cameron turned on the lantern after a while and checked his watch. "I'm going to see what we've got outside," he announced. He got up and opened the door. Sunlight streamed inside.

He returned a few moments later. "I guess St. Thomas got sideswiped instead of hit directly, but it sure was bad enough. Even if the car's operational, we'll play hell getting around with so many trees down. We'll have to stay here until the morning, maybe longer."

He picked up Selim's computer and went out into the wreckage that had once been a lovely, recently renovated bungalow. Tess and Selim followed. They left Bulgar in the closet.

The power was still off. Tess swiped all objects from the kitchen counter, set the small radio on it and turned it on.

"…devastation of St. Croix after a direct hit on the island. St. Thomas residents are asked to report to the hospital if medical help is needed. Otherwise, you are asked to remain where you are until cleanup crews can repair downed power lines. I repeat, it is dangerous to move about the island until damage is assessed and repaired."

"That's what I figured," Cameron said. "Let's see what we can do around here to make it livable. Selim, you're in charge of meals. See what you can do about scaring up something to eat. The stuff in the fridge should be fine for a while if we keep the door closed as much as possible. Tess, find more containers and drain as much water as you can get out of the pipes. I'll clear out some of this mess and board up what I can."

They ate cheese and fruit, washing it down with the last three cans of soda. They had canned food in the pantry and thawing prepackaged dinners left in the freezer. Tess figured they could survive on what they had for three or four days. By that time, but hopefully before then, it would be safe to leave the bungalow and find a way off the island.

"I'd better call and report in," she told Cameron. "Control will know where I am, and they'll be worried."

"You're chipped," Cameron said, guessing. He referred to the computer chips imbedded under the skin to transmit the coordinates of the agents in the event they were captured, killed or otherwise unable to communicate their location.

Tess nodded. "Of course. Aren't you?"

He shook his head. "Not anymore. Call then. We'll need to turn Selim and Bulgar over to the authorities. Maybe Mercier can get us a chopper in here."

She reached into her pocket. "My phone's missing. I must have dropped it in the closet." But she hadn't used it since calling Mercier from the air. Maybe she had lost it on the plane.

They quickly began a search, but the phone was nowhere to be found. Cameron offered his and she called Mercier.

Mercier assured her there would be a plane for them as soon as the airport in St. Thomas was clear. All available helicopters were employed in rescue efforts. She informed him that they had prisoners to deliver. He instructed her to get to the airport as soon as it was safe to travel and to wait there.

Tess rang off, gave Cameron his phone back and resumed her task of filling their empty plastic soda bottles with water from the faucets.

All day the three of them worked to restore what order they could to the borrowed bungalow. Tess and Cameron stopped periodically to check on their prisoner in the closet. Bulgar remained silent and sullen, apparently resigned to his fate. He wouldn't even deign to look at them.

"Is it all right to leave him in there?" Selim asked. "You're sure he can't get away?"

Cameron shook his head as he swept mud out of the kitchen. "He's not going anywhere until we take him to the airport."

"I don't like that he's not talking to anyone," Selim said. "He looks mad enough to kill."

"Cameron and I are armed, Zee. You're safe." Tess wasn't altogether comfortable in leaving Bulgar alone, either, but didn't see a better alternative. She changed the subject to distract Selim from the worry. "I haven't done this much housecleaning since I moved out on my own," she said with a laugh.

"I haven't done this much in my entire life," Cameron replied. "How about you, *Zee?*" he asked, a note of sarcasm in his voice when he used Selim's nickname for the first time. "You ever have to lift a hand to honest work?"

Selim held up a soggy sofa pillow and wrinkled his

nose. "Unfortunately, yes. I have lived alone for some time. My father threw me out when I was only a boy."

"You were nineteen and grown. Didn't see eye to eye with the old man, huh?" asked Cameron.

Selim didn't answer. Tess felt his sadness without even looking at him. He regretted losing his family by alienating them so badly and ignoring his father's warnings to shape up.

"You can fix things with your parents, Zee," she told him. "Write to them or call. I'll bet they'd be glad to hear from you. It's been years now, hasn't it?"

"Six." Selim tossed the spoiled pillow aside and took up another, picking leaves off it as if they were leeches. "I went too far, I think. My father is not a forgiving man." He worked on for a few minutes. "However, I am his only son."

Tess sensed a smidgeon of hope in him. "Give it a shot, why don't you? You'll have to do time, but you'll be in an American prison. Your parents might come to see you."

"No," Selim said with a sad sigh. "It would be too embarrassing, for me as well as them. Better if I leave things as they are. I am dead to them."

Tess knew he wasn't being completely honest in that. He would contact them soon; he was daring himself to do it even as they spoke. The intent was right there in his mind, plain as day. After last night's scare, when he thought they might be blown to kingdom come at any moment, his priorities had sort of shifted.

That made her wonder if she should take her own advice and call her own mom and dad. Maybe later, when the mission was over. Besides, she didn't even have a phone and wasn't about to borrow Cameron's to make a personal call.

But she thought about it. Her parents had loved her; she knew that. They still did, and she loved them as well. What point was there in resenting the way they had raised her? Or rather, how they had abdicated the responsibility for raising her and left her to her own devices?

Hadn't it worked? Hadn't she turned out more strait-laced and self-assured than she would have if they'd exerted authority over her? They had been little more than kids themselves when they'd had her and had had no parental role models to follow. When this was all over, she would call.

They continued their cleanup efforts until it grew late in the day. Now and then, Tess would stop, turn on the radio and get up-to-the-minute reports.

The devastation sounded horrific despite the fact that St. Thomas had escaped a direct hit. Flooding was rampant. The winds had destroyed many buildings, and trees and power lines were down all over the island, blocking roads. Injured victims crowded the hospital, and the airport was full of people demanding to leave the island.

They could hear helicopters buzzing overhead, further assessing the damage and performing rescues when signaled.

When the sun was low in the sky, Cameron, their self-appointed crew chief, called a halt to the cleanup. The bungalow was free of debris, though still damp and muddy in places, which would have to wait for a washing down.

Cameron had covered the broken windows with boards he had found stacked under the deck. These had probably been used in previous hurricanes to prevent the kind of damage sustained last night.

"Let's eat something before it gets dark and flip those mattresses," he suggested. "They've dried out some but will be dryer on the bottom."

Tess swiped her forehead with the back of her hand. "I'm just happy we don't have to spend another night in the closet, worrying about the rest of the roof flying off."

They slept in the bedrooms that night. In the larger bedroom Tess slept alone and Cameron made himself comfortable on a makeshift pallet of dry pillows and blankets from the closet. The two prisoners lay securely cuffed to the headboards of the twin beds in the other bedroom.

No one slept well.

It was mid-morning before they risked leaving for the airport as Mercier had ordered. Luckily the car had sustained nothing more than large dents and cosmetic damage. As they descended the hill, they saw and heard crews working near the roads, clearing away fallen trees with chain saws.

Cameron followed the winding Hull Bay Road, which intersected the road leading to Lindbergh Bay. He switched on the car's radio and tuned in the local news.

"…winds exceeding one hundred forty miles per hour caught St. Thomas virtually unaware, leaving residents with very little time to shore up for the storm. At least fourteen deaths have been confirmed. We expect that toll to rise when further reports become available.

"Damage to our town of Charlotte Amalie alone is still being assessed. Floodwaters are receding, but more rain is expected by nightfall."

The announcer continued with a plea for the inhabitants of St. Thomas to join in the rescue efforts in their immediate vicinity. He advised against any travel, but this was necessary.

"We're lucky we were on the north side of the island, and not right on the beach or on top of a cliff," Cameron said.

"Water across the road!" Tess cried, pointing as they rounded a curve.

They seemed to be on fairly level ground, so Cameron risked driving through it. He maneuvered carefully. "It's not far to the airport."

"I worry about securing Bulgar there until Mercier sends a plane," Tess confessed.

Cameron nodded. "Could be a problem. Maybe we can commandeer a room at a nearby hotel."

It began to rain again, raising the threat of further flooding on top of the awful devastation all around them.

Though a few foundations displayed no sign of the buildings that had topped them, most of the houses they passed stood in shambles, roofs bare of half their shingles or missing altogether. Windows had been blown out, and debris littered trees and yards.

The closer they got to the coast, the worse things were. Cars lay on their sides, upside down or smashed by uprooted trees.

"Looks like a war zone," Cameron observed.

The first hotel they came to was the Rillion-Marks, a modest three-story structure, which appeared to have survived nearly intact. Inside, the lobby was half filled with noisy refugees seeking a dry place to stay and tourists clamoring for the staff to find them a way off the island.

The clerks were harried and rumpled, as if they'd worked all night. They probably had. They seemed to be trying to vacate the lobby.

"Get a manager's attention and flash your badge," Cameron suggested to Tess. "I'll keep an eye on these two."

She found the right guy, who was arguing with a batch of tourists. He was saying, "I am so sorry, but all of you must go outside! The upper floors are being evacuated! There is structural damage to the hotel, and it is not safe…."

No sooner had he said that than screams emanated from a stairwell. Tess, trained to help rather than run from a dangerous situation, headed for the source of the screaming. The wall beside her buckled just as she reached the door marked Stairs. The door fell outward, trapping the lower half of her body beneath it.

Panicking crowds rushed out of the stairwell, feet treading on the door that half-covered her. Tess braced herself for death beneath trampling feet and the increasing pressure of the heavy door. Intent on protecting her head, she wriggled as close to the wall as possible. Suddenly half of the door's weight shifted as the door tilted like a seesaw, with her as the fulcrum. Irregular jolts shook her as the horde of frightened hotel guests thinned.

The ominous creaking from above grew louder. She could hear it well above the terrified shouts and screams of the escaping hotel guests.

"Cam?" She tried to scream his name, but it came out a near whisper. Any sound other than shallow breathing had grown nearly impossible. Maybe this was it, she thought. No energy left to struggle. "Mission's done," she muttered to herself. Cameron would wind it up. Grid was safe. At least she had done her part. Small comfort against the burgeoning pain and imminent burial beneath tons of concrete.

She fought panic, deliberately distracting herself with thoughts of Cameron and the wildly romantic night of love they had shared. Sex, really, but she could pretend it was love if she wanted to. She was dying here. She could think what she damn well pleased. Her shallow breath caught on a sob.

Can't lose it now.

Cam liked her, loved her, wanted her. And she could have saved him from himself, from his loneliness. *Nice pipe dreams. Yeah, right.* If only he could save *her.* Literally.

She bit down on her fist to control the panic. Tess tasted blood and wondered if she'd drawn it with her teeth or if something inside her was crushed. She tried to move the door from on top of her, but it wouldn't budge.

The ceiling above her cracked, raining plaster dust on her exposed head and arms. She closed her eyes and tried to hold herself together and not give in to terror.

Cam, where are you?

Chapter 13

Cameron tried to stand his ground as the mass of people panicked, pushing, shoving and screaming their way out of the building. He, Bulgar and Selim were about ten feet inside the front entrance. He jerked the prisoners to a corner on one side of the main doors and stood in front of them, shielding and guarding.

Man, how he wanted this to be over. He wanted Tess safely out of this mess and the mission finished and nothing preventing him from making his intentions clear. What would she think of that? he wondered.

There had been plenty of time to think while waiting out the storm. Tess made him want things he had never seriously considered before, like children, a house with a yard, a dog, holidays with family visiting. Things his mother had said she wanted for him. All of a sudden, he craved all that with Tess. His one driving ambition would be to see her happy, whatever it took. And he suspected she would be just as willing to put his needs first if he let her. Wasn't that what real love was supposed to be? But where the heck was she, anyway?

He searched the throng rushing past them but couldn't see her anywhere. His shout was lost in the cacophony. He did see the manager she had gone to speak with. The man wore a look of abject terror as he attempted to skirt the edge of the crowd and get outside. A number of other red-jacketed staff were doing the same.

The building was coming down. That was the only explanation for what was happening. He ought to get Bulgar and Selim to safety and hope that Tess had already made it out.

But Tess would not have gone without them. No way. She was still in here somewhere, maybe knocked down.

"Tess!" he shouted again, then tried to hear a reply through the many voices around him. He thought he heard his name, but maybe it was all in his head. At any rate, he had to find her.

He risked losing the prisoners if he did. Bulgar could escape and follow through with his threat to the power grid. Selim would surely disappear. The mission would fail. But he couldn't abandon his partner. No, Tess was more than that. More than a partner, more than a lover. He couldn't leave the building until he knew she wasn't in it.

He shoved the car key into Selim's hand. "Zahi, take Bulgar to the car. Lock yourselves in, stay there and wait for me. Do that and I swear I'll do everything in my power to get you the best deal possible. I have to find Tess. She might be hurt."

"Go!" Selim cried and grasped Bulgar by the arm, dragging him into the rush of fleeing people.

Cameron slid along the wall, fighting the tide of bodies. It was thinning even then. Dust and debris were falling from the ceiling, and he heard creaking sounds from above. Quickly, he scanned the floor and almost immediately saw the door off its hinges. And Tess beneath it, only her head, arms and shoulders visible.

He rushed to her, and with what seemed to take superhuman effort, he lifted the heavy door off of her. His fingers went immediately to her neck. He groaned with relief. She was alive. Strong pulse, but unconscious.

She shouldn't be moved, but he had no choice. They could both be crushed if they stayed. Without pausing, he lifted her in his arms and joined the last remnants of the fleeing guests of the hotel.

Cameron rushed to the car, his breath coming in heavy gasps. He managed to get the back door open and laid Tess inside. Bulgar and Selim were not there, of course. He hadn't really expected they would be. Later, he'd find them. For now, he had to get Tess to the hospital.

Then he realized that Selim had the car key. Cameron thought he had locked the car, but maybe in the rush, he'd forgotten. He quickly opened the glove compartment and found the valet key, stuck it in the ignition and roared away, pressing on the horn and dodging pedestrians. In moments he was racing toward the hospital, crashing through the hastily thrown-up roadblock barriers and bouncing through open ground around fallen trees.

The ER was a mob scene. Cameron carried Tess right up to the desk and laid her on top of it. "She was crushed by a heavy door and might have internal injuries. Please!" he begged. "Get a doctor!"

The receptionist threw up her hands. "I'm sorry, sir, but we have to—"

"I'm familiar with triage! She's critical. Get a doctor for her *now!* I'm a federal agent. Don't make me use my gun!" he warned.

The receptionist gulped, eyes wide. "Bring her this way," she said, her voice an octave higher. She pointed to the elevator. "Go up to X ray. Tell them Dr. Mellison sent you for a full-body scan." She punched the elevator button.

"If this is a trick to get rid of us, I'm coming back for you," Cameron warned.

"No! Just tell them. I'll notify the doctor and get him to meet you up there. It's a madhouse down here."

"Thanks," Cameron muttered as he got on the elevator. The receptionist stepped in, punched the correct floor and hopped out again.

Cameron uttered every prayer he knew on the way up, his eyes locked on Tess's face, hoping she would open hers. "Hang on, Tess. Just stay with me."

She groaned and moved in his arms. "Cam…"

"Shh. Just hang in there. We're on our way to X ray. You'll be fine soon, Tess. I promise you'll be okay."

She blinked up at him, and one corner of her mouth quirked up. "Knew you'd come."

"Better believe it. Now be quiet and save your breath."

His heart was thumping like mad, and he felt tears threaten as they stepped off the elevator.

* * *

A half hour later the doctor joined Cameron in the hallway outside X ray. "You're the lady's husband?" he asked.

"Her partner. We're here on government business. Is she going to be all right?"

The doctor nodded. "A couple of cracked ribs and some severe bruising to her left hip and shoulder."

"Are you sure? There was blood on her lips. Her lungs?"

"Are fine," the doctor insisted. "She got the breath knocked out of her. There are bite marks on her hand, and the blood's from that. She'll need some bed rest for a few days and a little TLC. We're full here. Do you have a place to take her?"

"I do. You mean she can leave? But she was unconscious!"

"She fainted and exhaustion took over. Her head is fine. No concussion. The tech is helping her dress, and she'll be out in a few minutes. Here," the doctor said, handing him a plastic bottle. "Pain meds. I doubt you can get a prescription filled with the way things are. Bring her back if she runs a high fever. A couple of degrees is nothing to worry about, though." He gave a quick nod of dismissal and turned to leave.

"Thank you, doctor." Cameron sank down onto the nearest chair and buried his face in his hands. Man, what a day. He had totally abandoned the mission. Tess would be furious about that, but he had to admit he wouldn't have done anything differently.

The door opened, and Tess emerged on the arm of the

technician. "Hey," she said with a grimace. "Sorry to give you such a scare. I was pretty scared myself, though." Then she looked around. "What did you do with—"

"They're gone," he admitted. "I'm sorry, Tess."

She dropped her shoulders and let out a sigh. "I'd better notify Jack. Maybe we can find them before they get off the island."

"It's been well over an hour and a half," he said as they walked slowly to the elevator. "They're long gone by now. Boats will be coming and going with rescue personnel. The ferry's probably running by now. They can get off the island any number of ways."

"But they don't have passports," Tess reminded him.

"They might. I left Bulgar's briefcase and the laptops in the trunk. Selim had the car key, and the car was unlocked when we got to it. I've been too busy to check yet, but I expect they took everything with them." He ran a hand over his face as he cursed. "Damn. There went our evidence, too. Well, if you're well enough, I guess we should head to the airport and wait for a plane."

"Maybe we'll find them there!" Tess said hopefully. "They might think we were trapped in the hotel or at the hospital."

"Wouldn't that be convenient? Not likely, but I guess it's as good a place as any to look for them, considering the hundreds of alternatives."

He helped her to the car and got her settled inside. Just as he went around to the passenger side, his cell phone chirped. "Cochran," he answered, so sure it was Mercier, he didn't even bother to look at the readout.

"Is Tess alive? Is she okay?"

"Zahi?" Cameron was astounded. "Yeah, she's all right. Where the devil are you?"

"Consider me a hero lost in the storm. I am no problem to anyone ever again. I vow this on the head of my precious mother. Oh, by the way, Bulgar is in the boot." The line went dead.

Cameron stared at the phone. Tess's number. So Selim *had* taken her phone. He'd been waiting for his chance to escape. "Slippery as an eel," Cameron mumbled.

"Was that Jack?" Tess asked when he opened her door again.

"No, it wasn't Mercier. Come on, I know moving is painful, but you have got to see this." He helped her get out and led her around to the back of the vehicle and opened the trunk. "I see it and I still don't believe it."

Bulgar lay on his side, his hands still bound securely behind him with the plastic restraints. His ankles had been tied together with his necktie, pulled up and secured to the wrist cuffs. He glared up at them, unable to speak even if he'd been willing to. Selim had gagged him with his own handkerchief.

"He left the computers, too!" Tess exclaimed with delight. "But the briefcase isn't here."

"There was cash in it. Are you surprised it's gone?" Cameron unzipped Selim's computer case. "So is Zahi's passport and ID."

Tess looked up at him. "We'll have to go after him."

Cameron raised an eyebrow. "I believe Zahi Selim was forever lost in the storm. At least that's what he *said* happened to him."

Tess sighed. "You're testing me to see if I'm capable

of bending the rules. I admit I'd like to let him go, but we need to find him and you know it."

"Yeah, I know." He untied Bulgar's feet and dragged him out of the trunk. "Let's get this one taken care of first."

Tess suffered every bump and jolt on the way to the airport. Her ribs ached abominably, and she felt as if her head were spitting. Cameron commandeered an unused conference room in the terminal and ordered a cot and pillow for her.

He first secured Bulgar to one of the chairs and then gave Tess the pain meds that he had gotten at the hospital.

"Get some sleep now," he ordered. "And as soon as you reach D.C., I want you to get to the hospital and get thoroughly checked out again. They were too rushed by all the emergencies here to suit me."

She agreed, touched by his concern. She watched as he settled at the table and began working on his computer. *Doing his post-op report,* she supposed. His powers of concentration amazed her. He had to be suffering an adrenaline crash. She knew *she* was.

Poor guy looked as bedraggled as she felt. They had all been soaked from the rain, splattered and half-coated by mud and then showered with plaster dust at the hotel.

Bulgar remained steadfastly silent, though she couldn't imagine he had anything to say that would help him. Cameron hadn't even tried to interrogate him, and she guessed there was little need for it at this point.

Three hours later Tess woke as Mercier entered the

room. He acknowledged Cameron with a nod, then went immediately to the cot. "How are you feeling, Tess?"

"I'll be all right," she said, sitting up with some effort.

Cameron had rushed to help her stand and did so gently as he spoke to Mercier. "She needs medical attention before you start debriefing. Are you flying directly to Washington?"

"The plane's ready." Mercier glanced at Bulgar. "Where's the other one?"

"Got away when the hotel was collapsing. He's probably found a way off St. Thomas by now, but I'll find him," replied Cameron.

"He's headed home," Tess said. "You have his parents' address?"

"How do you know that?" Cameron asked.

"He was thinking about reconnecting with his parents. Thinking seriously about it," explained Tess.

Cameron smiled. "In English?"

"Some things transcend language. I felt his need," she said.

"Ah, you could read his need." Cameron looked into her eyes. Neither of them said anything.

Mercier cleared his throat. "Well, if you're ready to board, we'll get out of here. Cochran, good work. Report when you have Selim in custody, and I'll give you directions for delivery and arrange your debriefing."

Cameron nodded. "I'll help Tess onto the plane if you'll bring the prisoner."

"No need for that," Mercier said and went to the door and opened it. "We're ready to go."

Clay Senate, an agent Tess had briefly worked with

before, entered and took charge of Bulgar. The fierce-looking Native American was twice the size of his charge and usually just as silent.

Danielle Michaels, the primary agent on Tess's last case, came in, too. They had a lot in common, and Tess considered her a friend. She grinned at Tess. "Girl, you could use a bath and a good dose of chocolate! We'll fix you right up on the plane." At Jack's direction, Danielle, who went by Dani, picked up the computers belonging to Tess and Selim.

Mercier put his arm around Tess and supported her with his other hand. "I'll take care of Tess." He spoke over his shoulder to Cameron as they headed out. "We need Selim's testimony. You know what's at stake."

Tess knew Cameron understood that Selim's eventual testimony was not the most crucial element involved in the capture. Cameron would have to bring Selim in to clear the shadow from his own record. This was a test.

She and Mercier might know full well that Cameron had not warned Selim two years ago and allowed evidence to vanish, but Cameron was still blacklisted, because some people did believe it.

Tess couldn't leave him without a goodbye. She knew Mercier didn't believe in goodbyes and wouldn't afford her a chance to say anything if she didn't insist. "Wait a minute." She stopped at the door and pulled away from Mercier's hold. "Cameron?" she said, suddenly at a loss for words. She didn't move any closer, afraid she would rush into his arms and betray the fact that they had been intimate. "Thank you," she said finally, hating how formal and impersonal it sounded. How inadequate. "For saving my life and…everything."

Cameron's eyes remained solemn. He wore a tight-lipped expression that spoke of resignation, lost hope and frustration. Then he nodded once. "You're welcome."

Mercier looked from one to the other, then embraced Tess again with his arm and ushered her out.

She wanted to burst into tears, to run back to Cameron, but managed to control herself. Hadn't she known from the beginning that the fantasy would end when the mission was over? Sure, Cameron had asked if he could call her after, but what good would that do?

Even if they didn't live so far apart, even if he got a job near her, they were so totally different that a real relationship would never work.

He had been making love to his invented Tess, not the person she really was. She wasn't even certain who *he* really was, and maybe that was what constituted her fascination with him.

She did know how sweet and funny he could be, how compassionate and how gentle when he tempered that fierce strength of his. He had risked his life to save hers. Twice. How could she not love him?

Chapter 14

Later, on the plane home, Dani joined her, bringing coffee and a sandwich. "Here you go, sweetie. Eat something, and then I'll help you freshen up a little."

"I'm okay," Tess said, forcing a smile.

"Not hardly. You're in pain and in love, neither of which makes you okay."

Tess sighed and took the coffee. "I didn't know you were an empath."

Dani laughed. "I don't have to be. You wince every time you move, and I saw your Mr. Cochran. Muddy and scruffy as he was, he looked like a heartbreaker. Your little farewell scene gave you away."

"Damn. You don't think he realized it, do you?" Tess asked.

"Are you going to eat that sandwich?" Dani asked,

avoiding the question. "At least try half of it." She took half herself and bit into it, probably to keep from having to answer.

Tess finished the coffee, unwilling to share anything about Cameron with Dani or anyone else. "Is Jack with Bulgar?"

Dani nodded. "You know Jack can't read him, though, and the man hasn't said a word since we got on the plane."

"He hasn't said anything since we took him down twenty-four hours ago except that he wants a lawyer."

"Really? Have you tried getting in his head?"

"No," Tess admitted. "We had plenty of evidence even before we caught him, and I figured he'd be mentally interrogated, anyway, once we got him squared away."

"Eric is on assignment and couldn't come with us for this. Jack, Clay and I don't have that skill. But you've worked with Eric on yours in the past few months. So Jack and I think *you* should give it a go now if you feel up to it, see if you pick up on something he might be ruminating about."

Tess knew she couldn't begin to do what Eric Vinland did. He was amazing, his ability incredibly reliable. "Eric says I try too hard and should just loosen up and let it happen. I wish it were that easy."

Dani sighed. "Well, I can't do it at all, and believe me, I've tried. Guess you either have it or you don't. I get premonitions sometimes. You know, flashes that often pan out. Do you get like internal conversations or what?"

Tess tried to explain it. "Well, you know how sometimes people talk to themselves out loud, sort of for emphasis or to hear the problem stated audibly? We tend to do that inside our heads, too. Those words I can get if I am focused on subjects and can see their eyes."

"Windows of the mind as well as the soul, huh?"

"Exactly. But some people rarely think in actual words, only in a jumble of impressions and emotions, usually too erratic to follow. Some who do internal verbalization do so in other languages, as Zahi Selim did in Arabic, his mother tongue. I could get his intent and his feelings, though, so he was a pretty good subject. It's exhausting when it does work, and I usually can't keep it up for long."

She thought of reading Cameron's mind the night they made love. That had been exhilarating.

Dani was tapping her lips with her finger as she thought about it. "Interesting. Why not go and sit with Bulgar, stir him up a bit and see what happens?"

"It might work," Tess said, thinking out loud. She had read Selim pretty well, and that had given her confidence a boost. She had gotten into Cameron's head a time or two, though only when he intended for her to do it.

It was certainly worth a try with Bulgar. He was probably too busy worrying about his fate to worry about guarding his thoughts. He wouldn't know that he needed to. And he'd probably be thinking a lot since he wasn't saying anything.

"Maybe I could ask some pointed questions to steer his thoughts," she told Dani. "But I'd feel a little more confident doing it if I felt human and didn't look like the wreck of the century."

"You're a trouper, kid. C'mon, we'll take ten and get

you decent. I've got makeup in my purse and a change of clothes in my carry-on. We'll fix you right up."

Forty-five minutes later Tess proceeded to do what she could with the brooding Bulgar. "Your attorney will meet with you after we land, but if you cooperate, it will only help your case."

Bulgar's chest ached. His fists hurt from clenching them. How had this happened? Had Eckhardt ratted? Or maybe Acton had. But neither of them knew where he was living. Selim had led these federal agents here to trap him. How had he known the location? He was just a tool, a second-rate hacker, a kid, for God's sake.

Somehow everything had fallen apart. Somehow they had traced him, but how?

"How long have you lived on Martinique, Mr. Bulgar?" The woman kept asking him these random questions, as if he would answer anything she asked. "You might as well talk to me. The evidence against you is pretty conclusive."

Did she take him for a fool? They had nothing on him. *Nothing!* Let them drag him back to the States. Let them check his finances, talk to his *wife*. There wasn't a speck of evidence anywhere that could link him to anything. All he had to do was keep his mouth shut, and they'd have to let him go eventually.

It would all fall on Selim; he had set him up and seen to that. Bulgar decided if he said anything at all, it would be to admit that Eckhardt and Acton had a grudge against him. He could say they were simply using him to deflect attention from *their* plan to shut down the grid.

Accusing him because he hadn't been around to defend himself. After all, they were the ones with access. What could he have to do with it? he'd ask. He had been gone from there for years! Best defense in the world and it would work, too. Neither of them had any proof of his involvement.

But for now, he wouldn't speak. He wouldn't say a word. He shot the female agent a look of disgust. She was government, the embodiment of everything he despised. Government, the Department of Energy especially, had wrecked his whole life. He would have the last word on this, that was for sure. Once they had to turn him loose, they would learn who held the power in his hands.

When Tess finished the one-sided interrogation with Bulgar, she left the prisoner and reported to Mercier. "Sir, I have two names for you. The first is Ekherd, or Ekhardt, something like that. The other is Acton."

"Do you know who they are and if they're related to the threat?"

Tess nodded. "Either formerly or currently employed by DOE. Currently, I think. Bulgar's planning to say they're pointing the finger at him."

"Motive?" he asked.

"Revenge against the government in general, most likely because they cut funds, and the Department of Energy in particular, because he was forced to leave it."

"You got all that? I'm impressed. Anything else?"

"He's still determined to do something, even if he has to do it while incarcerated, but he hasn't formed a backup plan yet. Hatred and a burning need for revenge on Selim are distracting him. I did what I could to increase that in order to keep him frustrated and his mind busy."

"Excellent." He began making notes.

"His thoughts are pretty repetitive. That's all I could get."

"Certainly more than we hoped for," he said with a smile. "There will be a commendation in this for you. You performed extremely well under unexpected and hazardous conditions. I'll admit, I would never have sent you in without a senior agent if I had known this much physical danger would be involved. To tell you the truth, because of your lack of experience, I figured Cochran would carry you on this, but you surprised me with your initiative and adaptability. Good work, Tess."

She blushed, warmed by the praise and a little embarrassed by it. "Cochran does deserve much of the credit, sir. He suspected all along that there was an insider running the show and Selim was only a tool."

Mercier pointed at her with his pen. "And you just discovered two more insiders. Valuable information we could not have gotten any other way. Vinland might have given us that once he returned to D.C. and interviewed Bulgar, but it could have come too late. So don't be modest."

Tess felt Cameron might get the short shrift, and she wasn't having that. "Cochran's experience in the field actually drove the investigation all the way, and he saved my life twice. I hope he'll be commended, too."

Mercier was busy writing again. "Of course. Now, take a break, Tess, get some rest and I'll get cracking on these names you gave me."

"You don't think Cochran's coming back with Selim, do you?" she asked Mercier.

In fact, she worried about that herself. Selim had kindly left them all the evidence, even the communications on his laptop that incriminated him. And he had called to assure Cameron that he was no threat. He was going back to Egypt to make up with his parents. Would Cameron let sympathy for the young man influence him?

Mercier was regarding her with an intensity that made her nervous. "I think," he said slowly and meaningfully, "that you are overly concerned about a former agent who is no longer your affair."

No longer your affair. That said it all, didn't it? Tess wished she could forget it, but she couldn't. Cameron had awakened something inside her and changed the woman she had been. He had given her his trust and earned hers.

Attraction, lust, respect, admiration, compassion as well as trust. All that almost equaled love, didn't it? Maybe if he had thrown in commitment, but it had been too soon for that, she supposed.

So what was she hoping for even if he did come back, even if he called her and wanted to get together again? He'd told her plainly that he liked what he did, fishing off the coast of Savannah. She would never fit in there. No hope they could have any sort of regular relationship.

"Let it go, Tess," Mercier advised.

"I didn't think you were telepathic, sir," she said with a sigh.

"I'm not. Just observant. It's hero worship, Tess, and misplaced at that, so get the stars out of your eyes. Cochran won't settle down. He never has."

Tess had no reasonable argument for that. The crushing ache in her chest had nothing to do with her injuries.

Cameron returned to the bungalow, picked up the baggage they had left there and drove back to the airport. It took several days to get a flight out of St. Thomas and make connections to Egypt.

He had no jurisdiction to arrest Selim once he got there. The Egyptian government had allowed the FBI and CIA to have former PLO official Mohammed Rashid a while back. He had been brought to Washington on board a secret U.S. military transport.

There had been no legal or court proceedings, no deportation procedure or extradition hearing. That told Cameron that Mercier could have effected Zahi Selim's extraction without any help. This was a test of Cameron's loyalty and willingness to obey orders, plain and simple.

He figured his only option was to convince the young man to return with him to the States and face the music. Now was the time Cameron certainly could use Tess's powers of persuasion, because if he were Selim, he'd stay put.

It took thirty-six hours and three plane changes to reach Cairo. That late in the evening was no time to approach Selim's parents and try to locate him, so Cameron checked in to a Novotel near the airport, ordered room service and planned to get a good night's sleep.

Every time he closed his eyes, he saw Tess. That sweet little body, so full of energy, so light in his arms. Those bright blue eyes searching his, giving up her own thoughts with every expression. He imagined he could smell the scent of her hair and her skin, the impressions imbedded in his brain when he'd made love to her.

He *missed* her. Had he ever missed anyone before? He had lived his life avoiding vulnerability. And involvement, he admitted. Maybe the two things naturally went together.

Also, for the first time in his life, he was apprehensive about his ability to do a job. How in the world could he get Selim to give himself up? How would Tess handle it?

Back in the world, Tess tried to resume life as usual. She wore her little gray suits and sensible shoes. She went to work precisely at seven, doing threat analyses and re-searching potential problems while she waited for another assignment. Her ribs had healed. Her heart had not.

She was in love with the man. Might as well admit it even if there was absolutely nothing she could do about it. Nothing she *should* do about it.

He had fallen off the face of the earth. No one had heard a word from him or Selim, unless Mercier was keeping it to himself.

She wondered if something terrible had happened to him in Egypt, assuming he had taken her suggestion and had gone there looking for Selim.

Bulgar was arraigned and charged, still remaining silent. The two men whose names Tess had gleaned were also taken into custody and, believing that Bulgar had given them up, related the plan as they understood it.

"So we don't need Selim," she told Mercier. "His tes-timony won't change anything."

Mercier paused, giving her that look that seemed a

reprimand for not recognizing the obvious. "Cochran needs him. You know why."

Six weeks later Mercier buzzed Tess to come to his office. She smoothed her skirt, tucked a strand of hair behind her ear and marched down the hall to the inner sanctum, hoping he had a new mission for her.

She had tried everything else under the sun to put Cameron out of her mind. Nothing had worked. She couldn't even bring herself to take him off her speed dial. How many times had she stared at that phone, willing it to ring? And how many times had she almost called him, only to remind herself that Mercier was absolutely right? She had to let it go.

"Come in, Tess," Mercier called when she knocked. "Someone is here to see you."

Her pulse leaped. *Cameron?*

Mercier gestured to the wingback that faced his desk.

Tess stepped forward and her heart sank. "Zee? I can't believe it! Where is…?" She stopped herself and rephrased her question. "When did you get here?"

Selim smiled as he stood and held out his hand to shake hers. "This morning. I have been giving a statement of my involvement. My father says it is an admirable thing to take responsibility for one's actions, even if they are wrong. So I have come."

Tess glanced at Mercier, wishing she could read his poker face. He had an ironclad shield up, a necessary thing, she supposed, when you worked with his kind of staff.

She wanted to scream, "Where is Cochran? What's

happened to him?" But knowing Mercier's assessment of her *hero worship,* she held her tongue.

Mercier smiled as if he approved of her decision to keep quiet. "In light of Mr. Selim's voluntary cooperation and invaluable assistance in the capture of Mr. Bulgar, I feel we should recommend that he be allowed to return to Cairo. Since you are better acquainted with him than anyone else involved, do you have any objection?"

Tess took a deep breath and shook her head. "None at all, sir. And Zee, I agree with your father. Stay admirable, okay?"

"Okay!" Selim said with a grin. "I have decided to enter the textile export business. Father believes I might someday become manager of his London market, when I have learned how everything works."

"Quite a gamble, Zee. I'm sure you won't let him down," she said, glad he was getting this second chance.

Mercier handed her a folder. "Here is your new assignment. Try to wind it up in a couple of weeks, in case something else pops and we need you back here."

She held the folder. "Any special instructions or information I'll need besides this?" she asked.

"All in there. Now get out of here and get busy. Mr. Selim and I have a few more things to discuss before I order his ride to the airport."

"Keep in touch, Zee," she said, shaking his hand.

Selim pumped hers hard, grinning from ear to ear. "I will, Tessa. And thank you for changing my life."

Tess smiled her goodbye, unwilling to say it out loud and thus ignore Mercier's tradition of avoiding the words. He seemed to believe it jinxed a return or something, and they all complied without ever discussing it. She did hope to see Selim again and wished him well in his new life.

Maybe she ought to thank Selim for inadvertently changing her life. If it had not been for him, she would never have had those days and nights as Tessa, the rich girl who shopped and partied on the French Riviera. She would never have met Cameron. She would never have fallen in love.

Even though it hadn't worked out for her and Cameron, Tess didn't regret a single second of it. She and Cameron had gone their different ways, but she had always known they would have to do that. She still had every larger-than-life minute of their time together, good and bad, to hold forever and remember.

She went back to her office to read the folder of instructions Mercier had given her so she could get on with the next assignment.

Maybe she looked the same as before and had resumed the regular routine of her life, but Tess knew she was forever changed.

Chapter 15

Cameron kicked back on the small deck of the *Lucky Duck*. She was a far cry from the yacht he'd captained in Saint-Tropez, but that was okay. Nothing could beat viewing the world from the flybridge of the *Duck,* hooking a marlin, snoozing in the little cabin on a cool afternoon. He had customized her so he could live on her if he had to. Nope, the upscale *Jezebel* didn't fit his lifestyle, anyway.

Neither would Tess, but he thought of her constantly and wondered if he'd ever see her again.

Maybe he'd give her a call and see if she would still give him the time of day. Probably not and what would be the point? Mercier had warned him off and given good reasons for it. Still, Cameron needed to hear her voice. He took out his cell phone, as he had so often since he'd returned to Tybee. It chirped in his hand.

Bobby Ray. "Hey, boss, we got a half-day fare up here at the café looking for a coast tour. I know you don't like to do 'em. You want me to take it?"

"I'm aboard. Send 'em on over." Cameron stuck the phone back in his pocket. One last customer of the season. What would he do all winter?

He glanced over at Café Loco, only faintly curious about who would want to go out on a cold day like this.

A figure in blue headed down the dock, strutting in high heels. His smile grew wider as she drew closer.

She was wearing a bright blue silk number much like the one he'd bought her in Nice. She must be freezing in that thing. The chilly breeze off the water teased the pale blond tendrils that had escaped from her upswept hair. What the hell was she doing here? And did he even *care* why so long as she *was* here?

She stopped next to the *Duck* and propped one hand on her hip. "Captain Cochran?" she asked with a sly smile.

"Agent Bradshaw." He stood up. "Getting late. I doubt you'll catch many fish before dark."

"What if I'm not fishing for fish?"

"Kick off your shoes and come aboard," he said, feeling like the gods had smiled at last. He reached for her and she leaned forward, her hands resting on his shoulders as he lifted her aboard.

The silk felt so smooth beneath his palms, her skin beneath it firm and cool. He caught the scent of her, even sweeter than he remembered. "You look incredible."

"And you look contented," she said with a sigh as he

held her. "I hoped to find you a little bored here after your travel and adventures. How was Cairo?"

"Crowded. Inconvenient. Not too hospitable. How's McLean?"

"Just the way you left it when you brought Zahi back. Why didn't you stop by and say hello when you were there?" The question sounded casual, but he knew it wasn't. Her feelings were hurt.

"Mercier didn't think it would be a good idea."

"I know he offered to take you on. Not interested, I guess."

Cameron let her go and stood back, taking her hand. "Let's just say he sounded less than enthusiastic. I guess there's still that little black cloud remaining. I'm okay here."

"Oh, he wants you all right. He sent me to persuade you."

Cameron resented that. Tess should have come on her own because *she* wanted him, and he thought at first she had. "So I'm your current mission, huh?"

She smiled and squeezed his hand. "For the second time around. Do I have any chance of getting you off this boat and back to your old life?"

He pursed his lips and studied the creek's outgoing tide, which was seeping back to the Atlantic. "How much time do you have to work on it?"

"Couple of weeks."

He sighed. "It could take that long. I'm fairly dug in here. Stubborn as I can be, too. Everybody says so."

"And *I'm* fairly persuasive," she warned. "I had lessons from the best in how to entice a man to do something."

She removed her hand from his, padded barefoot over to the companionway and peeked inside. "Not too shabby. I could work in these conditions."

Cameron felt almost giddy about her doing just that. However, noting the ease with which she got around the deck without wobbling or turning green, he also experienced a little guilt over how she was able to do that. "There's something I probably ought to confess. About your seasickness, or rather the way you overcame it."

She turned and made a dismissive gesture with her hand. "Oh that. You hypnotized me, of course."

"You were aware of it? I must be losing my touch."

"No, but I have thought about it a lot since then, replayed what went on in the restaurant that day. It finally came to me how you did it."

"And you're not mad that I did?" He could hardly believe it.

"No, I don't mind. As a matter of fact, when I told him, Mercier was really interested that you could do that with so little prep and without my knowledge or cooperation. 'Valuable tool,' he said. Also he likes that you're a believer. You know, in what some of us on the team are able to do. Like my telepathy. That's improving, by the way."

She ducked inside the cabin and sat down on the bunk where he spent most of his nights.

He followed her in. "So you can read my mind now?"

"Sometimes I get a glimmer of what you're thinking, but I believe it's only when you want me to." She bounced on the bunk a couple of times as if testing its comfort quotient.

"You did great reading Zahi and, from what Mercier said, Bulgar, too."

"Thanks." She patted the bunk beside her, and he sat down. "I hear Savannah is steeped in paranormal stuff," she said. "You ever try to delve into that?"

Cameron shook his head, distracted by the way she looked, sitting there on his bunk, leaning back on her hands, her head quirked as she gave him that seductive smile he had once encouraged her to use on someone else.

"I did study it to some extent just to see what it was all about," he admitted. "You can't grow up around here with all the ghosts and things without getting a dose of Geechee culture and hearing about the voodoo."

"So you learned how to cast spells." She sat forward, as if fascinated. "That's basically what hypnosis is, right?"

"Well, I don't know if I'd say they're the same. With spells, the trick is that the caster and the castee both have to believe in it. Seriously believe. Then it works."

"You believe in the spell you've cast on me?" she asked, leaning closer.

"Do you?" He drew a finger across her brow and down the side of her face, ending at the edge of her mouth.

"Seriously believe it," she admitted, looking breathless with anticipation. Her lips were parted.

He trailed the finger down her neck and let the tip of it rest on the swell of her breast. "I wonder who's doing the casting here."

"Using every trick you taught me and then some," she admitted. "Are you under now? Can I command you to move to Virginia?"

"Not yet," he said, moving closer to feather teasing

kisses across her lips. "Mercier gave you two weeks. Don't spoil him by reporting success too soon."

"Then I am succeeding?" she said, catching his mouth with hers.

He kissed her again, tasting her gently and pulling back when she would have deepened the kiss. "Too soon to tell. Remember, you're supposed to enjoy your work. Why rush through it when you don't have to?"

She moved his hand to cover her breast. "You're toying with me."

"Any objections?"

"None whatsoever," she said and lay back on his bunk and watched with slumberous eyes as he undressed her.

He thoroughly enjoyed the view of her lying there as he did a quick version of the strip he'd done for her before. Her slow, seductive smile grew wide.

Maybe she hadn't come to Tybee just to repeat the job offer, after all. He moved onto the bunk with her, taking her in his arms. "You feel so good," he whispered.

"I feel just great," she said with a shy laugh. "I missed you, Cam."

"I missed you, too." He smoothed his palms over her back, her sweet little behind, and pressed her close as he kissed her hard. *Game over.* He didn't care if she knew how desperately he wanted her. Or how little restraint he had left.

She opened to him immediately and sighed her feeling when he entered her. For a long moment, he held still, savoring the oneness, wishing it could last forever.

Right then he knew without a doubt. "I love you, Tess," he whispered.

Her body responded, moving beneath him, demanding everything and giving everything without hesitation. Vaguely, he registered that she hadn't said she loved him, but he felt it with every brush of her hands, in her kiss and in the wordless sounds of pleasure she made as he loved her.

Urgency wrecked his control, his wish to make it last, and seemed to fuel her own response. He thrust faster and faster until he felt her tremble and contract around him. He groaned with release and sheer exhaustion.

And he couldn't help a tinge of disappointment. This should have been sweeter, longer, more romantic for her. This was the woman he *loved,* not some quick roll in the hay. Hell, their first time had gone smoother than this. He had never lost control this way.

He moved off of her, lay on his side and cuddled her close. "Next time…"

"That was wonderful!" she mumbled, her words vibrating against his shoulder. "*You* were wonderful."

She meant it, too; he knew she did. Cameron smiled and nuzzled the top of her head, planting a kiss there on her tangled curls. "I love you, Tess. If you love me, too, will you stay with me? Marry me?"

Her sigh warmed his skin. "You have two weeks to persuade me, and this was a pretty good start."

"Do you think you could love me?" he asked seriously, holding her tighter, needing the words.

She moved her head so she could see his face. Her heavy lidded gaze met his. "Read my mind. Of course I love you. Why do you think I came down here? I wouldn't have exposed half my boobs in that tarty dress or put those arch-killing shoes back on for anybody but you."

Cameron laughed and kissed her forehead. "No reason to go to all that trouble. I was a goner when you came down the dock the first time."

"Liar! I was a mess that day!" She laughed and rolled her eyes. "You thought I was a frump. And I was."

"You were as cute as a little buttoned-up agent could be, but I never place much stock in looks. Do you? Those are far too easy to change and disguise who you really are."

"The way you changed mine. I came here like that to persuade you, but you do realize that I'm not really a 'sexy blue silk and do-me shoes' kind of girl, right? I thought maybe you made me into what you wanted."

He tapped her chest with his finger and smiled into her eyes. "It's this Tess inside I fell for. Brave, sweet, unpredictable and pretty damn smart. Beautiful Tess, inside and out." He rested his palm over her heart. "Can't live without her."

"You know this is moving way too fast?"

He didn't think so. "We are both trained to make quick decisions, though."

"True," she agreed. "And to trust our instincts." She pondered for a minute. "But we should base the decision on the facts available. The books all say that."

"Ah, gotta go by the books. That's my Tess."

She hummed and nodded. "Too many people rush into marriage without any pertinent information about each other. For instance, I don't even know what religion you are. I'm Methodist."

"Retired Catholic," he replied.

"Republican or Democrat?"

"Republican. Sometimes Independent. You?"

"Democrat."

"Uh-oh. You root for Georgia or Tech?"

She wrinkled her nose. "I hate football."

"Want kids?" he asked.

"Do you?" Now she looked worried, so it must be important to her, one way or the other.

Maybe this Q and A wasn't such a bad idea, after all. He had never really thought much about fatherhood, except to prevent it. But now, with Tess, he realized he did want children. Very much. That surprised him a little.

"I do, Tess. Eventually. Maybe when we decide to get out of the field and into desk jobs. Five or six years maybe?"

"I'm good with that. What about finances? You're a big spender. I'm pretty frugal. Looks like we don't have much in common."

"Makes it more interesting, don't you think? If we agree on everything, we don't argue. We don't argue, we don't get makeup sex. I hear that's the best kind."

She laughed. "Better than this?"

"We'll see."

"You're definitely interesting, Cochran. But I am *so* not your type," she warned, tugging gently on his chest hair with two fingers.

"I'm not yours, either, but what the hell? Will you marry me, anyway?"

"Yeah," she growled, laughing softly as she wriggled even closer and slipped her arms around him. "What the hell. Now, about that next time you mentioned…"

Epilogue

"You're *what?*" Mercier had nearly shouted the words.

Tess had moved the phone away from her ear. She could never recall hearing him lose his cool before. "I'm getting married. Any of y'all want to come for the wedding?"

"Are you out of your mind? Tess, you don't *know* this man."

But Tess did know him, and she had told Mercier so in no uncertain terms. In fact, she had convinced him beyond a doubt before the call was over. He had accepted that and moved on to inform her that she and Cameron would be placed on different teams and could never work missions together or simultaneously, but she understood that was policy.

Mercier and several of the other agents, including her

matron of honor, Dani Michaels, came to the wedding. It was a small evening affair in Cameron's parents' church in Savannah. The ceremony had been short and sweet, and they were now celebrating the reception at his parents' lovely old home right down the street from the church.

Her parents were here, too, beaming with pride even though they hardly knew the woman she was and had never understood her. She loved them, anyway. Being in love herself had made Tess realize the radical change they had made in their lives in order to give their baby a decent chance at a normal life and good education.

Cameron's mom and dad had warmed to her right away, seeing her as the reason Cameron was finally settling down. Cameron's years lying about Tybee and fishing had given his father reason to rejoice in the job his son had now.

Tess had even accepted his mother's offer of her wedding gown, a lovely ivory satin number that fit perfectly. It made her feel as glamorous as the blue silk had in Saint-Tropez. But underneath, she wore sensible two-inch heels as a concession to her practical side. She was who she was.

Cameron swept her into their first waltz as the three-piece orchestra played Strauss. He wore a tux the way he wore everything else he put on, with casual elegance and supreme self-confidence. She loved that so about him, even though he did let her see his vulnerable side now and then. She loved that even more.

"Are you happy?" he asked as they twirled about the floor of what had been a ballroom well over a century ago. The man danced the way he did everything else.

"Deliriously happy," she admitted, smiling up at him.

Later, they waved goodbye from the horse-drawn carriage that would take them to the picturesque hotel where they would spend their wedding night and three-day honeymoon. Then it would be back to the office and future missions.

What a fantastic November day, unusually warm right into the evening hours. Perfect and so memorable, their wedding day. The horse clopped along at a lazy pace, seeming to mock their eagerness to be alone together after the long day of excitement and anticipation.

"I love the way Savannah's lit up," she said as they completed their ride through the historic district of the beautiful old city, checkered with unique homes and lovely little parks.

"She's my home, this old city."

Tess smiled at Cameron as he helped her out of the carriage. "And she has electricity because we helped save the power grid. Doesn't that make you feel good, having a hand in that?"

He grinned happily as he accepted the key card at the desk, offered his arm and escorted her across the hotel lobby. "I feel great about it. And we should definitely celebrate that," he declared, employing his slow Southern drawl. "I know. We'll make love all night with the lights on!"

She blushed and looked around to see the other patrons and staff smiling at them. "Is making love all you think about?" she whispered.

"Well, no, but it sure beats the hell out of fishing!" With that, he scooped her up in his arms, ignored the open elevator and carried her up the polished wooden staircase, just like in the movies. Miss Scarlett O'Hara had nothing on her!

Chameleon that he was, with an ability to fit into any given location or situation, Tess *knew* him. Deep down, beneath everything from scruffy sea captain to suave sophisticate, lay this teasing rogue, the real Cameron Cochran.

And he was all hers. She could see it in his eyes.

* * * * *

"AREN'T YOU GOING TO SAY 'Fly me' or at least 'Welcome Aboard'?"

Amanda Bauer didn't. The softly muttered word that actually came out of her mouth was a lot less welcoming. And had fewer letters. Four, to be exact.

The man shook his head and tsked. "Not exactly the friendly skies. Haven't caught the spirit yet this morning?"

"Make one more airline-slogan crack and you'll be walking to Chicago," she said.

He nodded once, then pushed his sunglasses onto the top of his tousled hair. The move revealed blue eyes that matched the sky above. And yeah. They were twinkling. Damn it.

"Understood. Just, uh, promise me you'll say 'Coffee, tea or me' at least once, okay? Please?"

Amanda tried to glare, but that twinkle sucked the annoyance right out of her. She could only draw in a slow breath as he climbed into the plane. As she watched her passenger disappear into the small jet, she had to wonder about the trip she was about to take.

Coffee and tea they had, and he was welcome to them. But her? Well, she'd never even considered making a move on a customer before. Talk about unprofessional.

And yet…

Something inside her suddenly wanted to take a chance, to be a little outrageous.

How long since she had done indecent things—or decent ones, for that matter—with a sexy man? Not since before they'd thrown all their energies into expanding Clear-Blue Air, at the very least. She hadn't had time for a lunch date, much less the kind of lust-fest she'd enjoyed in her younger years. The kind that lasted for entire weekends and involved not leaving a bed except to grab the kind of sensuous food that could be smeared onto—and eaten off—someone else's hot, naked, sweat-tinged body.

She closed her eyes, her hand clenching tight on the railing. Her heart fluttered in her chest and she tried to make herself move. But she couldn't—not climbing up, but not backing away, either. Not physically, and not in her head.

Was she really considering this? God, she hadn't even looked at the stranger's left hand to make sure he was available. She had no idea if he was actually attracted to her or just an irrepressible flirt. Yet something inside was telling her to take a shot with this man.

It was crazy. Something she'd never considered. Yet right now, at this moment, she was definitely considering it. If he was available…could she do it? Seduce a stranger. Have an anonymous fling, like something out of a blue movie on late-night cable?

She didn't know. All she knew was that the flight to Chicago was a short one so she had to decide quickly. And as she put her foot on the bottom step and began to climb up, Amanda suddenly had to wonder if she was about to embark on the ride of her life.

HARLEQUIN® *Presents*®

AT HIS
Service

From glass slippers to silk sheets

Once upon a time there was a humble housekeeper.
Proud but poor, she went to work for a charming and
ruthless rich man!

She thought her place was below stairs—
but her gorgeous boss had other ideas.

Her place was in the bedroom, between his
luxurious silk sheets.

Stripped of her threadbare uniform, buxom and blushing
in his bed, she'll discover that a woman's work has never
been so much fun!

Look out for:

POWERFUL ITALIAN,
PENNILESS HOUSEKEEPER
by India Grey
#2886

Available January 2010

www.eHarlequin.com

New Year, New Man!

*For the perfect New Year's punch,
blend the following:*

- *One woman determined to find her inner vixen*
- *A notorious—and notoriously hot!—playboy*
- *A provocative New Year's Eve bash*
- *An impulsive kiss that leads to a night of explosive passion!*

When the clock hits midnight Claire Daniels
kisses the guy standing closest to her, but
the kiss doesn't end after the bells stop ringing....

Look for

Moonstruck

by *USA TODAY* bestselling author

JULIE KENNER

Available January

red-hot reads

REQUEST YOUR FREE BOOKS!

2 FREE NOVELS
PLUS
2 FREE GIFTS!

ROMANTIC SUSPENSE

Sparked by Danger, Fueled by Passion.

YES! Please send me 2 FREE Silhouette® Romantic Suspense novels and my 2 FREE gifts (gifts are worth about $10). After receiving them, if I don't wish to receive any more books, I can return the shipping statement marked "cancel." If I don't cancel, I will receive 4 brand-new novels every month and be billed just $4.24 per book in the U.S. or $4.99 per book in Canada. That's a saving of 15% off the cover price! It's quite a bargain! Shipping and handling is just 50¢ per book in the U.S. and 75¢ per book in Canada.* I understand that accepting the 2 free books and gifts places me under no obligation to buy anything. I can always return a shipment and cancel at any time. Even if I never buy another book from Silhouette, the two free books and gifts are mine to keep forever.

240 SDN E39A 340 SDN E39M

Name	(PLEASE PRINT)	

Address		Apt. #

City	State/Prov.	Zip/Postal Code

Signature (if under 18, a parent or guardian must sign)

Mail to the **Silhouette Reader Service**:

IN U.S.A.: P.O. Box 1867, Buffalo, NY 14240-1867
IN CANADA: P.O. Box 609, Fort Erie, Ontario L2A 5X3

Not valid for current subscribers to Silhouette Romantic Suspense books.

Want to try two free books from another line?
Call 1-800-873-8635 or visit www.morefreebooks.com.

* Terms and prices subject to change without notice. Prices do not include applicable taxes. N.Y. residents add applicable sales tax. Canadian residents will be charged applicable provincial taxes and GST. Offer not valid in Quebec. This offer is limited to one order per household. All orders subject to approval. Credit or debit balances in a customer's account(s) may be offset by any other outstanding balance owed by or to the customer. Please allow 4 to 6 weeks for delivery. Offer available while quantities last.

HARLEQUIN® HISTORICAL:
Where love is timeless

From chivalrous knights
to roguish rakes, look for the
variety Harlequin® Historical
has to offer every month.

www.eHarlequin.com